HIDDEN PROMISES

MARIE HARPER WRIGHT

Digital ISBN: 978-1-7399307-2-1

Paperback ISBN: 978-1-7399307-3-8

Jack,
My best friend, my husband, my rock.

CHAPTER 1

Sophie Ward opened her eyes wide, letting the make-up artist swipe her long lashes with mascara. It was all fake—well, her eyelashes anyway. She had never needed to wear so much make-up in her life. But then again, she had never been to such a big event either. And she had no doubt that of all the occasions to go full glam, this was *the* event where false eyelashes were an absolute must.

Just please don't make me look like a clown. She hadn't been able to see herself in a mirror yet and had spent well over an hour in the chair. Her bum was getting numb. Katie, her make-up artist, moved onto her lips, concentration etched on her face.

"You done with the eyes now, honey?" Matt, her hairstylist, asked Katie. He'd been sitting on the edge of the bed in the hotel room, waiting till Katie was finished with Sophie's eye make-up before continuing with her hair.

Sophie was thankful. She didn't want to get stabbed in the eye while he tugged at her locks. He moved over to her and started messing with her hair again.

As nice as it was to be pampered, it was starting to get on her nerves. How did celebrities do this all the time?

Katie drew on lip liner, a much deeper shade than Sophie would ever choose for herself. *Yep, I'm definitely going to look like a clown.* The liner tickled Sophie's lip and she desperately wanted to scratch.

The hotel door opened and her best friend Belle walked in, carrying a takeaway tray of drinks for them all. Belle stopped in the doorway, staring open-mouthed at her friend. Sophie's eyes widened. *Oh God, please don't tell me I look a state.* Searching her friend's eyes, she desperately tried to understand what Belle was seeing.

"Wow, Soph, you look incredible," Belle breathed. Still gawping at Sophie, she put the drinks on the table.

Thank God. Sophie relaxed into the chair a bit more. Belle would never lie to her.

"You wait till you see her in her dress!" Matt told her. "She's going to outshine all those celebrities without a doubt." He carried on pulling at her long blonde hair.

Belle handed Sophie her iced tea. She had got Sophie a straw so she could sip without ruining her make-up.

"Can I?" Sophie croaked and lifted her cup to Katie. She was desperate for a drink.

"Course." Katie straightened up and took her own drink from Belle.

Desperate to quench her thirst, Sophie sucked at her iced tea, relishing the sweetness. Her hand shook slightly, the ice in her drink clinking together. As Matt and Katie drank and chatted to each other, Belle bent down to Sophie, taking her hand in hers and squeezing. "Honestly, you look absolutely beautiful."

"Not like a clown?" Sophie whispered.

Belle shook her head, her deep brown hair swishing from

side to side. "Not a red nose in sight," she joked, and straightened up.

Katie looked at her watch. "We haven't got long. Sophie, did you want to have a little walk around and use the toilet before we finish? Then you'll need to get your dress on and we can do the final touches before you leave."

Glad to finally stand up, and sure her usually pert bottom would now be flat with all that sitting, Sophie went to the bathroom, desperate to look herself over. Locking the door behind her, she took a calming breath and looked in the large mirror above the sink.

Her breath escaped her. *Wow*, she did look amazing. Matt had pulled her naturally blonde hair to one side and given it a soft curl. It was simple, but so glamorous. No wonder it had taken an hour to perfect. She marvelled at her eyelashes. They didn't look fake or over the top at all. Her eyeshadow smouldered and her cheeks were a perfect peach hue. Even with just red lip liner on, she knew this would be the most beautiful she had ever looked.

Ten minutes later she was ready to don her outfit. There had been several choices, but she just couldn't resist the opportunity to wear a deep emerald green silk number. It was as if the dress had been made just for her, as if she were a movie star. The soft fabric skimmed her hips and dropped to the floor, pooling like an oasis with a small train behind her. The deep v neckline showed off her ample cleavage and meant she needed tape to ensure she didn't spill out. There was no way she could wear a bra with it, so they had given her the slightest bit of padding built into the dress.

But it was the back she loved the most. The fabric of the straps cascaded down her sides and then joined together just at the top of her bum, exposing her whole back to the world.

Belle helped her put her nude, strappy, six-inch heels on. Her feet would kill by the end of the night. She was used to working in flat pumps—there was no way she would be able to teach and look after thirty children every day in anything else. She was so out of practice with heels that she'd had to practice walking in them around her living room.

At last, she was ready. Her hands shook holding the little clutch bag that matched the colour of her dress perfectly.

"Wow," they all breathed when she turned around and examined herself in the mirror.

"That arsehole better not stand you up," Belle said, her mouth pursed together in a tight line.

They didn't talk about Scott anymore. It just ended up with Sophie defending him and Belle getting upset. He wasn't a reliable boyfriend and he had stood her up before. But Sophie hoped he knew how much tonight meant to her and would be on his best behaviour. Plastering a fake smile on her face, she hid her worries.

"Why didn't he come and get ready here? That's what normally happens," Katie asked, touching up Sophie's lipstick for the hundredth time.

Sophie shrugged while Belle turned round and muttered, "Exactly."

Scott had said he didn't want to get in Sophie's way and would prefer to get ready at his home and meet her there. What could she say? She could hardly beg him to get ready with her and admit how nervous she was about this whole thing.

She felt so out of her comfort zone, and not for the first time, wished she hadn't entered the damn competition. It was a moment of pure madness. She still didn't know what had made her do it. She'd been flicking through a copy of *Trending* magazine in the staffroom at Winton Green Primary School, where she worked, when she spotted the competition. And in a flash, she had visions of getting all dressed up, having a night out in London and finally doing something crazy. Something no one would have ever expected her to do. Having an experience she would never get again. So she'd entered, certain that her infamous ability to never win anything would prevail yet again. But the universe seemed to have other plans for her.

"You look beautiful, Sophie. Honestly, you'll smash this. I just know it." Matt squeezed her shoulders and combed invisible hairs into place. She had only met Matt and Katie in the past couple of hours, but they already felt like friends. Her team. Her entourage.

Sophie smiled. If she wasn't careful she'd turn into a diva.

Josh Heart hated these things. You were herded around like cattle, led from one journalist to the next, posing on the red carpet, flashing lights blinding you and unseen faces shouting your name.

Then when you were inside, the endless networking, the jostling and small talk did his head in. It was business, not fun. And it was necessary, he knew that, but it was a part of his job that he hated. He just wanted to get on with writing and singing and leave all this for someone else. But he couldn't. Everyone wanted a bit of him and no one else would suffice.

Blowing out a frustrated breath, he composed himself, rolling his shoulders back. Then he opened the door of his chauffeured car and emerged into the madness. Bright lights flashed around him, journalists and paparazzi called his name, and his fans screamed behind him in the darkness of the night.

Josh loved his fans. After all, they were the ones who bought his music and had made him who he was today. He always took the opportunity to give back and make them feel he cared for them. Because he did.

Turning his back on the red carpet in the chilly London air, he headed for the waiting crowd, mostly young girls and women screaming his name, waving at him to come to them. He signed autographs on pages and clothing thrust at him, and took a few selfies. Five minutes of his time was nothing for him, but meant everything to them.

Then he reluctantly retreated, waving and smiling at them, trying to maintain his smile as he returned to the waiting cameras and the red carpet. One wrong look and he would be breaking news tomorrow, with stories that he was a sulky celebrity, egotistical and demanding.

None of it was true, of course. But they didn't care. They could make you and they could break you.

He was directed to his mark on the red carpet, where he placed his hands in his trouser pockets. The dark grey suit fitted him to perfection, tailor-made for him just for tonight. He would never wear it again. The wastefulness of it irritated him, so he got his PA to sell off the clothes he couldn't wear again and donate the money to charity. The suit jacket stretched across his broad shoulders and his bright white shirt opened at the collar. He couldn't bring himself to wear a tie. It made him feel even more suffocated.

Giving the sexiest smile he could muster—the one that had helped him win the sexiest male award a few years in a row— he looked this way and that until he was directed to his next marker.

When his time was up, he was moved on to the journalists. He knew most of them from previous award ceremonies. It was best to keep them on his side, so he always made sure he was courteous and gave them time.

"Josh, you're wearing a Roguish Gentlemen suit tonight, is that right?" Pamela, the first journalist, asked.

"Yes, I am. I think they'll become a fashion powerhouse in the coming months. Just watch this space." He smiled down at her as she checked her notes, her bright red glasses sliding down her nose. Normally he didn't pay any attention to designer labels, but there was something about the soft, moveable fabrics and laid-back style that had appealed to him. And tonight was a good night to support a new and upcoming British designer.

"Are you looking forward to tonight's ceremony? Are you hopeful you'll win an award?"

"The Best of British Talent Awards ceremony is the highlight of the awards season. It's great to celebrate British talent in all areas of entertainment. I'm up against some great acts tonight, so I don't think I'll win any of the awards, but I'm always grateful for being nominated and getting the opportunity to celebrate everyone's achievements." He was a humble man by nature, so he hoped people saw him as genuine and not just saying those things for good publicity.

"We think you have a great chance of taking home an award, Josh. We also know that you're meeting with one of our competition winners." She shoved the microphone back in his face to capture his answer.

"That's right. I'm very excited to meet her. Actually, I'm probably already late."

"Well, we'll let you move on. Good luck for tonight."

"Thanks, Pamela. Enjoy."

He moved on to the next journalist, ready to answer the exact same questions.

Sophie stood at the end of the red carpet, tucked away next to the building, her hands sweating while she stood...waiting. Alone.

She checked the time on her phone again. Scott was thirty minutes late and no text. She finally let her heart sink.

What an arsehole. Yet again he had let her down. How could someone she'd been with for so long keep hurting her? How could she keep letting him get away with it?

Tears welled in her eyes, threatening to spill. She blinked them away—she would not ruin her make-up.

Melanie walked back over to her again. She worked for *Trending*, the magazine that Sophie had won the competition with. The two of them had been in contact for weeks now, liaising about details for the night, organising the hotel room, hair and make-up, and her outfit. They had grown quite friendly.

"Still no sign?" Sophie saw the sympathy in Melanie's eyes. She shook her head, unable to speak due to the lump in her throat. Melanie squeezed her arm gently. "What do you want to do?"

There was no judgement, but Sophie still felt embarrassed. She couldn't believe he'd done this to her…except she could. This wasn't the first time he'd stood her up. It wasn't even the second. Scott liked to bail out on almost anything that she organised for them to go to together, whether it was a work event or a friend's party. Why had she thought tonight would be any different? Because she had finally told him how much it meant to her for him to be there with her? She shook her head at herself. She was an idiot.

"I'll do the pictures and the piece for you, and then probably head home," Sophie said.

The magazine wanted to run an article on the night and she didn't want to let them down, but she couldn't stand the thought of spending the whole night on her own with total strangers surrounding her.

Her skin prickled. Scott had known how nervous she was about this whole thing. And he still didn't care enough about their relationship to show up or to support her. Maybe she should start listening to her friends and her big brother. He really was wasting her time.

"I understand. Look, I probably shouldn't be saying this, but if you really don't want to be here, I can make up an excuse for why you had to leave."

Sophie shook her head. "No, honestly, that would make me feel worse." She wasn't one to throw kindness in someone's face, and the magazine had gone above and beyond for her. She would repay this small kindness at least.

"Okay, well, the offer is there if you want it. Are you ready to get this started or do you want a minute?"

"No, I'm fine." She tried to convince herself as much as Melanie.

"Okay, let's go this way. We have a little photo shoot set up and we can get some of the interview done." Melanie led her across the red carpet and through a side door into the theatre. As Sophie followed, the crowd shouted and cameras flashed. A new celebrity had obviously just arrived.

CHAPTER 2

Josh had finally finished with his interviews. Saying his goodbyes to the last journalist, he was then directed to meet Melanie. She was the organiser of the competition that had been run in *Trending* magazine, where the winner got to attend the award ceremony, have a photo shoot and meet with him for twenty minutes or so.

"Are you okay to start then, Mr Heart?"

Josh hated when people were formal with him. He was just a normal guy, but people didn't see it that way.

"Please, call me Josh," he replied, straightening his cufflinks—the only thing he was wearing that wouldn't be auctioned off. They had been an eighteenth birthday present from his parents.

"Well, Josh, this way please." She directed him to a side room of the theatre, where they had set up a photo shoot. "Sophie has just started her shoot. Are you okay to jump straight in?"

He nodded and walked over to the set, repeating Sophie's name in his head so he didn't forget it, still fiddling with his cufflinks as he walked.

When he looked up at the competition winner, his heart skipped a beat. The most beautiful woman he had ever seen stood in front of the camera, looking like a glamorous movie star. Her long blonde hair was styled to the side, and her luscious lips were painted red and pulled up into a shy smile at the camera. Her green dress hugged every curve of her body. He felt a tug against his trouser zipper at the sight before him.

He ogled her for a moment, committing every curve to memory—and every flutter of her eyelashes, the way her hair glistened in the lights, her nervous smile at the camera—before they were introduced. It was the best minute of his life.

Melanie stepped forward and spoke to Sophie quietly. Sophie nodded and the shy smile was replaced with an apprehensive one.

Then Melanie introduced them. "Sophie Ward, this is Josh Heart."

Utterly taken by her deep blue eyes, Josh stepped into the photo shoot and walked over to her. "Pleasure to meet you, Sophie." He brushed his lips against her soft cheek and kissed her, one side and then the other. Her hand clasped his arm for support. The camera clicked away.

"No, thanks for meeting me." Her peach cheeks darkened and her long eyelashes fluttered.

"Congratulations on winning the competition." He placed his hands in his pockets. The last thing he needed was to be pictured with a hard-on.

"I'm never lucky with those sorts of things. I never win anything." She spoke with such excitement, Josh found himself taken by her enthusiasm.

"I'm never lucky either," he replied, smiling. Apart from this moment right here—right now he felt like he was a winner, too.

Melanie interrupted with a small cough. "Sophie, could we

maybe do a lipstick touch-up and then the photos of you two together?"

Sophie nodded and followed her into the darkness. As she turned, Josh had to stifle a groan at the sight of her naked back, the most exquisite thing he had ever seen. Two dimples were nestled at the base of her back, her skin smoother than silk.

Melanie returned to him. "Just a heads-up, she's been stood up by her boyfriend. He was meant to meet her here but hasn't shown up."

"What?" Josh said, louder than he had intended. The photographer looked up at him and Josh smiled back, covering up his outburst. "Who would do that?" he said, a bit quieter this time. *And who would do that to someone like her?*

"I don't know." She shrugged, looking back at Sophie, who was with a make-up artist. "He sounds like a jerk, to be honest. Anyway, just thought you should know. She's here all alone, bless her."

"Alone?" His hands fisted in his trouser pockets.

"Yes, she said she's going to leave after this."

Sophie was making her way back over to them.

"She can't do that. She belongs in there, looking like that."

Melanie shrugged. "She doesn't want to be alone."

"Melanie, have her seated next to me. I'll look after her all night so she isn't alone."

"You don't have to do that. You only signed up for twenty minutes."

"I want to. You can sort it, can't you? She shouldn't have to leave just because of him. You heard her, she said she never wins anything." He didn't know why, but the injustice of it all stung him.

Sophie joined them but hung back, looking between them both.

Melanie muttered, "I'll sort it." She gave Sophie a small

smile and then left them, already typing furiously on her phone.

~

Even though it was happening at this very second, Sophie still couldn't believe she was meeting Josh Heart. Admittedly meeting him wasn't the reason she had entered the competition, but it was definitely a bonus. Who wouldn't want to meet the most eligible bachelor in Britain? He had become a British institution—his songs were everywhere on the radio and he'd been releasing hits for over ten years now. She had to admit, even just looking at him was some sort of payback for Scott having stood her up. Maybe this next fifteen minutes could make up for her whole night being ruined.

"Right. Are you both ready?" the photographer called out from the darkness behind the lights.

They had been taking photos for about twenty minutes before Josh arrived, and his handsome smile seemed to make the whole world stop spinning. She had just stopped feeling self-conscious and was getting into the swing of things when Melanie introduced them. Now she could feel her skin flushing pink every time he looked at her, and she would have to get her lipstick reapplied soon if she didn't stop nibbling at her bottom lip.

She went to stand with him, her pulse racing. Josh Heart was a heartthrob, she'd known that. Man, everyone in the world knew that. But all the pictures she'd seen didn't do him justice. He was a work of art. His black hair, the colour of the night sky, was swept back, not a strand out of place. His emerald eyes, flecked with deep amber like a tiger, glinted in the studio lights as though he was ready to devour his prey. But it wasn't just that. Every time he looked at her, her insides seemed to melt and her mind went all fuzzy. Thankfully Melanie had introduced them, because Sophie was sure he would have made her forget her own name.

The photographer directed them to stand next to each other. Even though she was wearing high heels, Josh towered over her. He must be a foot taller. His aftershave wrapped around them, clinging to every part of her body. It was probably the most expensive scent she would ever smell, a mixture of spice and wood.

As the photographer started taking pictures again, the camera clicking loudly, worry started eating away at her, infecting every part of her body yet again. She shouldn't be here. She couldn't stand up next to celebrities like Josh Heart, couldn't rival their beauty and poise. No matter how long she had spent in hair and make-up, no matter what dress she wore, she couldn't compete. These pictures would be disastrous. There was no doubt in her mind that she would be cropped out and left on the cutting room floor.

A warm hand slid along her lower back, taking her out of her pit of worry. She looked up at Josh, who was looking down at her, his piercing emerald eyes staring through to her very soul.

"Are you okay?" he whispered, barely moving his luscious lips, a slight smile tugging at the corners for the pictures.

"I just don't fit in here," she whispered back, not quite getting the knack of talking and smiling at the same time like he had.

The pressure of his hand on her back held her tighter. Reassuring her. "Of course you do. You're just new to it all. What do you do for a living, Sophie?"

The way he said her name made her heart skip a beat. His minty breath touched her skin as he spoke.

"I'm a primary school teacher," she breathed.

"Did you feel comfortable on your first day teaching the

children?" he whispered. "Standing in front of the class, all eyes on you?"

She shook her head. She'd been so nervous the first day of standing at the front of the classroom on her own, responsible for thirty children. But they didn't seem as scary as all of this.

"And to them, you are a celebrity," he said. "I bet if they see you outside of school they come flocking to you, calling your name, wanting to speak to you, and then tell all their friends they saw you?"

Sophie laughed. Yes, they did that. Not just her class, but any pupil in the school. Sometimes she had to duck and cover behind a shop display to avoid being seen.

Josh's eyes lit with delight, his full lips lifting at the sides. "See, you're probably more famous than I am."

"Actually, you're right. I think I'm *way* more famous than you." If she could get through that first day of teaching, she could get through this. Somehow Josh had taken all of her worries and handed back her confidence. She pulled her shoulders back and her smile brightened. Who would have thought standing next to a celebrity could feel so normal? Now he just seemed like an ordinary person.

Then the photographer wanted another pose—for them to stand side by side but Josh facing the back of the set and Sophie facing the camera.

Sophie tried to argue that Josh was the celebrity here, shouldn't he be front and centre? But the photographer just muttered something about the magazine piece being about Sophie's makeover and experience, and something about artistic flair.

"Josh," the photographer called out from behind his camera, still snapping away. "Can you please take Sophie's left hand, and place your left hand on her other hip?"

Josh did as he was instructed, skimming her hip and taking her hand. Sophie's heart fluttered. The tiniest touch felt huge.

Heat flowed from his hand through the thin silk fabric of her dress.

"Josh, bring your hand up as if you two are dancing a waltz," the photographer shouted.

Josh did as commanded, wrapping his fingers around hers. Sophie's nerve endings seemed to come alive as if electricity coursed through her body.

He pulled her closer, their sides touching, his firm chest next to hers. Snuggling his head against hers, his breath cascaded down her neck, sending goosebumps across her body. Her nipples tightened. *God, please let these bra cups be fit for purpose.*

"Relax, Sophie."

His words washed over her and at his command her shoulders dropped, her head rested against his and she melted into him. Living the lie for just one more second. Memorising this moment where she was the centre of his world. Being this close to him, being held so tight, was the safest she had ever felt, as if everything was right in the world.

She looked up at him through hooded eyes, her breath hitching at their proximity. His tiger eyes captivated her. If he just leant down to her—just a bit—he could kiss her. Claim her as his.

Movement and calling around them brought her out of her trance, and she snapped her head round to the commotion. The photographer had stopped taking pictures and crew members were dismantling the lights. Josh held her still, paying no attention to the movement around him. His attention was all on her.

"That wasn't too bad, was it?" His voice was hushed, husky.

Shaking her head slowly, she was unable to break away from his gaze. Bringing her hand to his hard chest, he bent his head lower, painfully slowly, inching closer to her. His eyes were now bright green, his lips slightly parted.

He was going to kiss her. Oh my God, Josh Heart was going to devour her, right here, in front of everyone.

She almost whimpered with need as fire ran through her veins, unable to move even if she wanted to. He inched closer, almost at her lips. And then his head twisted slightly and she felt his soft lips press against her flaming cheek.

He'd been going to kiss her. He had. There was no way she could have misread that. Was there?

He brought his head to her other cheek, his lips sinfully close to hers. If she just leant forward she would be able to taste him. And then he kissed her other cheek.

"Let's get you to the party." He tightened his grip on her hand and spun her around like a princess, breaking the tension between them instantly.

CHAPTER 3

Reluctantly letting Sophie's hand slide from his, Josh instantly missed their connection. What had got into him? He was never touchy-feely with a fan—it could get you into all sorts of trouble. He knew that from personal experience.

The sound of her heels clicked alongside him as he directed her across the marble floor to the foyer. There was the award ceremony first, followed by a sumptuous five-course dinner. He had no doubt that Melanie would be able to negotiate moving Sophie to sit next to him. They'd worked with each other before and she wasn't someone you said no to. She may have been small but her temper was mighty.

"Josh?" Sophie squeaked behind him.

He turned back to where she'd stopped behind him, providing her with his undivided attention. Her crystal-blue eyes were the colour of the ocean, and her hands twisted at her little bag.

"Sophie?"

There was something about this gorgeous specimen of a woman that called to him. He was drawn to her, wanting to bring her to him and wrap his fingers in her silky locks.

"I'm actually going to head home." She looked down at her perfectly manicured fingers.

This was no surprise to him, but he still couldn't allow it. "You don't have to leave, Sophie. You deserve to be here." He understood, he really did. He hated going to these things too.

"I just don't feel comfortable here alone. I told Melanie I'd do the magazine bits and then head home."

"You aren't alone. You have me." He tipped her chin up to look at him. Her heart-shaped face was perfection. She went to argue some more, but he said, "Sophie, you're with me. You can't go home yet. You spent what, a couple of hours in hair and make-up?" She nodded slightly, her eyes wide and innocent. "So then you should spend at least a couple of hours here having fun." He offered her his arm, not waiting for an answer.

Sophie's small hand curled around his bicep and he led her to the commotion. He would show her a good time, like she deserved.

As they sat together in the audience, listening to the award speeches, Josh was more aware of Sophie than anyone else. Acutely aware of her thigh an inch from his. Of her shoulder pushed lightly against his arm in the tight seating. The coconut fragrance of her hair tickling his nose.

"Now for the 'Best of British Male Singer-Songwriter' category," their host spoke out across the crowd of celebrities.

Josh bounced his knee up and down. He hated these things, he really did. But he'd be lying if he said he didn't want to win, the competitive side of him bubbling in his belly.

They sat and watched the reel of nominees and the song they were nominated for. It was a hard category. Lots of new singers were breaking into the business and he felt old. He'd been in the charts for fifteen years now, since he was twenty-one years old. Sure, the money was still rolling in, better than before probably. He was a British icon now, always on the radio, known worldwide with sold-out tours. But the egotistical musician in him needed this award. Needed this confirmation he still had it, that he could still compete, that he was still relevant. He hated admitting it. But it was true.

"And the winner is…" Josh waited, breath held, keeping his face as neutral as humanly possible. It was the longest few seconds of his life. "Daniel Sampson."

Applause exploded around the theatre and Josh's hopes shattered in his heart. He'd honed the art of losing awards now, trained his face to not show the disappointment he felt from head to toe. Trained himself to clap gracefully, a small smile on his lips, congratulating the winner.

Cameras pointed at the losers, hoping to catch them out. Not today. He clapped, staring straight ahead, dead inside. A realisation dawned on him. Maybe this wasn't for him anymore. Maybe he needed to retire. Maybe he was irrelevant.

As Daniel Sampson walked up the stairs to accept his award, the cheering and clapping died down. Josh shifted in his seat, wiping his sweaty hands down his thighs. *Fuck,* he screamed silently to himself. *This is bullshit.* He wanted to escape, knowing the next few hours would be filled with people offering him their commiserations, pity swimming in their eyes, their kind words of condolence—meant to offer him comfort at his time of pain—piercing his soul.

Everyone better fuck off. He wasn't sure if he'd be able to keep his anger in check tonight. He needed to write, to get it onto paper, rather than letting it escape in some other way.

Daniel Sampson started talking—some shit about how grateful he was. Josh drew in a shuddering breath. *Count to ten. One…two…three…*

A small hand twisted around his fingers, gripping them

tightly as if holding onto them to save his life. He looked down at the manicured fingers, the tension leaving his shoulders, melting away into the ground, his breathing slowing and the ringing in his ears stopping.

He looked up at their owner, not caring if the cameras were trained on him. Sophie sat, staring intently at Daniel talking on stage. Her face was as expressionless as his should be. As if she wasn't guiding him off the edge of a rooftop.

She squeezed his hand again, her thumb brushing back and forth over his knuckles, her eyes still trained on Daniel. Josh took the strength from her to use throughout the night and looked back at Daniel just in time for him to finish his speech and receive his final applause.

Sophie's hand left his to clap. And Josh was able to do the same, that same small smile returning to his face.

Shit. He was in trouble here.

CHAPTER 4

Food appeared, as if by magic, carried high by hundreds of waiters weaving their way around the large, round tables in the banqueting hall.

Sophie had never seen such an exquisite space. Ornate, gold carvings adorned the ceilings, large mirrors hung around the hall and spectacular chandeliers cast their light across the room. The chatter of the diners rumbled constantly, broken by an occasional glass clinking or a hearty laugh.

She sat next to Josh, caught up in the luxurious atmosphere. She savoured every moment, committing it to memory. Every part of tonight had so far exceeded her expectations. When Scott had stood her up she'd been adamant there was no way she'd be able to survive the night on her own. And now, not only had she survived, but she'd actually enjoyed herself. It was like she told her students—sometimes you just need to try something new, and who knows what amazing experiences you could have.

Their table of thirteen was being served their first course. The menu, also gilded in gold, noted they were to be served a homage to the potato and onion. *Creamy buttermilk mash, with potato puff and truffle oil, a puffed onion airbag, pomme soufflé and baby onion petals.* She was sure it would be lovely, but it did sound an awfully posh way of saying potatoes and onions.

Josh was surrounded by his closest allies in the business. She wasn't sure if they were actually his friends, or merely colleagues…or maybe his entourage. But whoever they were to him, he seemed more at ease with them than he was when the award ceremony ended and people came up to talk to him.

Then, Sophie had seen his jaw clenching, his eyes narrowed. He spoke kindly and calmly, swiping away any comments that he should have won, or how gutted he must have been. But somehow, she could tell it hurt more than he was showing. And even though she could see his pain through the shield he was trying to put up, he was a gentleman to her, introducing her to fellow celebrities and people in the industry, never leaving her out of the conversation, making sure her drink was always topped up and she was always by his side. It was surreal that he was so down to Earth, so normal. It was easy to forget he was *the* Josh Heart. Instead he was just Josh.

While they were waiting to hear who had won the award, his angst had pulsed from him. And when the winner was announced, she'd felt the air harden around him. Not able to help herself, and wanting to make him feel at ease like he'd done for her in the photo shoot, she had reached out to him, all the time keeping her eyes on the award winner so no one would be drawn to Josh and his loss. She'd hoped he would feel some comfort from her, and when he'd squeezed her hand back, she knew he had.

Now he was speaking to his manager on his left, his face chiselled to perfection as if carved from marble. Sophie had been introduced to everyone at the table, but she knew she'd forget everyone's names. They were all here for Josh and she was acutely aware that she was out of place, almost certain she shouldn't be sitting next to him, squeezed in between him and a representative from his music label. Surely she should have been seated away from all the celebrities, on the outcast table? But here she was, eating potatoes and onions five different ways. Thankfully, the food was the best she'd ever tasted. Which wasn't saying a lot. She was, after all, used to eating school dinners virtually every day of the week.

A hand slid along her back, bringing her out of her eating bliss. She turned to Josh, his fingers caressing her exposed skin, the friction of his touch another delicious memory she'd try to hold onto.

"Thanks for back there," he whispered, leaning closer to her.

"I didn't do anything."

"You really did." He continued stroking her back in lazy little circles, as if he wasn't even aware he was doing it. "Are you enjoying yourself?"

She nodded. "The food is incredible." She pushed around a tiny morsel on her plate, avoiding his hungry eyes.

"Sophie?" She looked up at him. "I'm sorry. Everyone thinks they own me, everyone wants to talk to me and tell me that I should have won the award, or ask me how I'm feeling. But all that craziness should be done now. Or most of it, anyway. Now we can relax, and we can have fun."

Her cheeks burnt hot. "Josh, please don't worry about me. This is your night. I'm not even meant to be here. I was only meant to be twenty minutes of your time." She shrugged and laid her fork down, losing her appetite. An uneasy feeling was settling in her tummy, one she didn't understand. But there was something about knowing her night was ending with Josh. Knowing that he probably didn't want to be here with her, and it was just a work obligation. It stung. And it stung way more than when Scott had stood her up. Surely that said it all?

Josh lifted her chin, capturing her eyes with his. "You're here because I wanted you here. Melanie told me you'd been stood up and I thought you deserved better than that."

Sophie's heart hit the floor with what she was sure would have been an audible *thunk*. She turned from him, dislodging his trailing fingers from her back, avoiding looking into his eyes which she was sure would be filled with pity.

She'd thought Josh just liked her, enough to spend some more time with her at least. How stupid she was. Of course a celebrity like Josh Heart didn't want to spend time with her. He was just being nice, probably for some good publicity. She didn't belong here. And she never would. She wanted to run.

"So, Sophie, what do you do for a living?" the man sitting beside her asked. She tried to remember his name. Christian. She plastered a smile on her face that she didn't really feel.

"I'm a primary school teacher." She had never felt so out of her depth. He was the record label representative.

"Really?" He raised his fluffy black eyebrows towards his slicked-back hair. "My wife is a primary school teacher too. I don't know how you ladies do it."

Sophie was aware of Josh shuffling behind her, but she ignored him. Instead she replied, "It can be tough, but it's what I've always wanted to do. Probably not as interesting as your job though?"

Christian went to open his mouth, but before any words came out, Josh cut in. "Sorry Chris, I've just spotted someone I wanted to introduce Sophie to. Do you mind?" He stood up without waiting for a response, trying to take her hand with him.

She wrenched it from his grasp. "Really, don't worry about that," she said. "I'm happy just staying here."

"Sophie…please?" He held his hand out for her to take, his eyes resembling those of a puppy begging for a treat.

She sighed. She always had been a sucker for good

manners. Her students knew how to get around her just like that too.

She got up and Josh led her through the tables, his grey suit jacket tight across his broad shoulders. When they entered the foyer again, he turned to her, stopping her in her tracks.

"Sophie, I didn't get Melanie to organise for you to sit next to me the whole night because I felt sorry for you." She bristled, her shoulders tensing. "I did it because I felt you deserved better than that. You obviously wanted to be here, otherwise you wouldn't have entered the competition. And then you were considering just going home. All I wanted was for you to have a nice night." He tilted her chin up again, his tiger eyes flashing. "Do you believe me?"

She nibbled her lip. Maybe she was overreacting. She'd spent so many years with Scott walking all over her and letting her down that she was assuming Josh was doing the same thing. Maybe he was just being nice.

"Yes," she croaked.

A bright smile lit his face. "Good. Then let me show you a good time." Taking her hand, he twirled her around, her dress billowing around her as she spun. A squeal of pure joy escaped her lips.

It was nearing the end of the night. Josh had never had so much fun at an awards ceremony. Apart from that one moment of doubt, Sophie had enjoyed every aspect of the night, her eyes twinkling as she smiled at the waiters carrying the five courses of Michelin star quality food, laughed with joy at her goodie bag of designer brands, and listened intently to everyone. Which went down particularly well with his manager, who was always looking out for a fresh pair of ears to listen to his stories about celebrity antics.

There was no doubt Josh succeeded in giving her the best night possible. Probably better than she would have had if her good-for-nothing, piece-of-shit boyfriend had shown up.

Hopefully ex-boyfriend now. He stroked his cheek, where stubble was starting to sprout in the late hour. He was glad he'd convinced her to stay, even if he did have to bend the truth and say that he only wanted to show her a good time. Sure, that was part of the reason. But the other part, which he'd hidden from her, was that he just didn't want to see her leave. He didn't know why, he just wanted more time with her.

Now Sophie was sipping her coffee, talking with Christian again about his wife and working in education.

She fitted in with his crowd. She fitted in with this world, rivalling all the top models in beauty. And yet she was so down-to-earth and caring.

He reached out for her again, unable to stop himself from stroking her bare back. Claiming it as his own. Little goosebumps appeared on the areas he traced and yet she kept her eyes focused on Christian.

He shouldn't be doing this. He shouldn't be doing any of it. She was a fan, he had to remember that. She was off-limits and he had to stop touching her. And he certainly had to stop thinking about kissing her, making her forget the world, running his hands through her blonde hair.

He couldn't do any of that. He didn't allow himself to be with fans anymore. That was his rule. And it was there for a reason.

Sophie stifled a yawn. They'd have to leave soon. And then what? He wasn't quite ready to part from her. They had already learned they were both staying at The Regent. He'd taken the penthouse suite for a few nights while his house was undergoing some renovations. He wasn't sure he'd be able to sleep knowing she was five floors below him.

God, she was like an itch on his back that needed scratching. It was just because he'd told himself she was off-limits. That's why she was becoming so irresistible to him.

Another little yawn escaped Sophie, her red lipstick still managing to have stayed put.

"I think, Cinderella," he whispered into her ear, "that it's past your bedtime."

"Spoilsport." She smiled back at him, her eyes hooded, looking eager for sleep. "But I think my fairy godmother is right."

They said goodbye to Christian and the few other stragglers left at their table. The majority of people had left over an hour ago.

The hotel was just a short walk away, so they decided to exit through one of the side doors. Hopefully there would be no paparazzi posted there so they could walk together. A member of staff poked his head round the door for them, to check the coast was clear. The paps must have all been waiting at the entrance, as they were given the nod that it was safe.

Walking with his hands in his pockets, Josh was thankful that the late summer night air was quite warm and Sophie wasn't feeling the cold. London still buzzed around them, black taxi cabs zooming along the road, street lights glaring and strangers passing by without a glance in their direction.

"Did you have a good time?" he eventually asked, breaking their comfortable silence.

"The best." Sophie kept a good pace with him in her heels, but he slowed to make sure she didn't twist her ankle. How tall would she be without them?

"I'm glad I managed to succeed."

A rowdy group of men walked past, and Josh stepped closer to Sophie to protect her from the stumbling drunks.

"Did you have a good night?" she asked him as the drunken calls died down.

"Well…apart from losing the award, putting my foot in it with you and spilling my dinner down me…yes. I had the best night ever." He wiped at the dark brown stain on his suit, some sort of jus that had been drizzled all over the main course.

Sophie chuckled at him. "Serves you right for shovelling food in your mouth." She elbowed him in the ribs. He loved that she obviously felt so comfortable with him. It had been a long time since someone had treated him like a normal guy.

Then her face turned serious, her eyebrows pulling together as she looked down at the pavement. "I think I was just being overly sensitive, you know?" She sighed. "I didn't want to feel like you pitied me."

"Did you pity me for losing the award tonight?" He hoped to God he'd read her right and this wasn't about to totally backfire.

Her frown deepened, and her nose scrunched up in disgust. How could someone manage to be cute and sexy at the same time?

"Of course not. You're a grown man; you can live with the disappointment of not winning. I just wanted to ease your worries and make you forget about it."

"Well, that's how I felt with you. I just wanted to be there for you, to help you forget. Even just for one night." He shrugged, resisting the urge to take her face in his hands and kiss her. He wanted more than one night, and that was becoming an issue.

"Well, you did. So thank you." She fiddled with her bag. Sophie looked like she wanted to say more but she refrained. Instead, she looked up at The Regent hotel, her expression thoughtful. "I should've known he'd stand me up," she muttered. "I don't know why I thought he'd be any different tonight. I've spent most of my adult life trying to make it work with him. How could I have been so stupid?"

Josh couldn't bear hearing her blame herself. He couldn't imagine her doing anything to justify being treated like this. He turned to face her, stopping just one inch away from her. Her eyes widened and her lips parted.

"This isn't your fault, Sophie. Don't you ever think it is. If that fool of a man doesn't realise what he's lost tonight, then he doesn't deserve you. Never has and never will." He stroked her smooth hair away from her neck, exposing it to the night sky. Tracing her pulse point with his thumb, he desperately wanted to taste her pale skin. She tilted her head slightly, inviting him to touch and suck.

But he had rules.

He shook himself from his daydream and stepped away from her. This couldn't happen. He needed to get her safely to her door and leave her there. In one piece. Safe and protected. From him and his world.

CHAPTER 5

Sophie had been sure Josh was going to kiss her neck, lick and bite his way up to her ear, suck her earlobe before kissing a trail along to her lips. And then devour her right there in public, tasting her, pushing his tongue into her mouth.

Well...that was what she'd hoped he was going to do, anyway.

Instead, he retreated. Physically and mentally. He stepped back, and those green tiger eyes that had devoured her and stripped her bare before him had great big iron bars in front of them. He was going to deny them both.

He rammed his hands in his pockets and turned on his heels, avoiding her eyes. She hurried after him, her feet throbbing.

Not saying a word to her—or even looking in her direction—he pushed the call button for the lift. She let him brood in peace, needing some space herself. After all, she did technically still have a boyfriend. One she was about to dump as soon as she got to her room.

When the doors closed on them in the lift, the air stiffened around them. Josh leant against the back wall of the lift, his hands still stuffed in his pockets, and let out a deep sigh.

Sophie pressed the number ten for her floor and settled back, clutching her bag in front of her as protection. Something was happening here, something she didn't understand. The lift trundled up at an excruciating pace, the tension increasing around them with every inch they rose.

After a decade, the doors dinged open and she left the lift, turning to thank Josh for a wonderful evening. But, to her surprise, he followed her.

"What?" he asked when he saw the shock on her face.

"I was just about to say goodbye. I thought you'd be going straight up to your room."

"A gentleman always walks a lady to her door." He studied her face for a moment. "Is that okay?"

"Y-yes," she stuttered. "Of course." Grabbing her key card from her purse, she walked the short distance to her room, number 115.

Sliding the key card into the lock, she waited for the green light to show before removing it. She let herself in and turned to him in the doorway. His silent form filled the door frame, brooding. Did he want to come in? She hadn't done this in so long that she didn't know the protocol anymore. Part of her wanted to invite him in. The other part was scared as hell.

"Thank you for tonight. I had the most wonderful evening. I'll never forget it." She nervously gripped onto the door handle.

"My pleasure." He didn't move. Before she could fill the void in their silence, he carried on, "Sophie, may I have your number please?"

"M-my phone number?" she stuttered again, completely shocked that someone like him would want her number.

His eyes squinted slightly, before he nodded.

"Of course," she replied.

He grabbed his phone from his pocket and handed it to her. As she typed in the digits, her fingers trembled. Once programmed in, she returned the phone to him, their fingers brushing ever so slightly. He checked his phone and typed on it, then her bag buzzed.

"There," he said. "Now you have mine too."

She wasn't sure what was happening, but felt certain she was about to wake up from a dream.

"Thank you, Sophie," he added.

And with that, he bent down to kiss her cheek, his lips searing her skin, then swiftly withdrew.

She couldn't watch him leave, so she shut the door behind her, banging her head lightly against it in case he heard.

Now that he'd left, she knew that she had actually wanted him to stay.

Finally kicking her heels off to ease her aching feet, she grabbed her phone. She had a job to do.

It was time for her debacle of a relationship to end. Taking a deep breath and dialling Scott's number, she stood in front of the mirror in the hotel room. She would never look this good again, she was sure of it. Even on her wedding day, there was no way she'd look this glamorous. And he'd missed it. He'd abandoned her in her time of need, when she had been open with him about her nerves and needing his support. Maybe it wasn't important to him, but this was the final straw. Scott had never been there for her, and until tonight she had never realised how toxic their relationship was. It was never going to progress, it was never going to get better. He had walked over her every minute of their long relationship. And now…enough was enough.

She waited for him to pick up. It was midnight, but she had no doubt he would answer. He was always up till the early hours of the morning.

"Hey, babe." Scott's cheery voice erupted from the mobile phone.

She took another calming breath, staring herself in the eye in the mirror, commanding herself to be brave. "Do not 'babe' me, Scott. You know why I'm calling. You ditched me tonight…again. How many times can you stand me up? How many—"

"Woah, babe. Calm down."

"I will not calm down. I've given you enough chances, enough years of my life. You knew how much I was worrying about tonight, and you couldn't even show up for me. Or even have the decency to tell me you weren't coming."

"Ah, man…was that tonight?"

His attempt at being blasé rubbed her up the wrong way even further. "Don't even try and pull that. We texted earlier on today and you told me you'd be there."

"Oh…yes," he fumbled. "I remember now. Babe, it's just that I wasn't really feeling well."

"What?" His change in tactic fuelled the fire burning within her. "God, I cannot believe I've wasted so many years of my life on you! Everyone around me warned me that you were playing me, that you would never treat me right. Every time, I defended you."

Just then, in the background, she heard a voice. "Yo, Scott, do you want another beer?" Scott tried to shush his friend but there was no covering it.

"You're with Ted, aren't you?" Before Scott could try to muster up another lame-arsed excuse, Sophie did what she should have done years before. "It's over, Scott. You're a piece-of-shit boyfriend I never should have given the time of day. I don't want to hear from you again, do you hear me? Don't you dare think you can grovel your way out of this one. I'm done." And before he could respond, she hung up.

The silence rang in her ears. She expected to feel a stab to her heart, her gut to wrench, tears to fall. But as she stood there in her emerald green dress, she was calm, unfazed and at peace. The only pain she felt was in her feet from her shoes that night. The only tears that wanted to be shed were tears of relief at being free.

She had done it.

Finally.

And she had never felt better.

CHAPTER 6

After a long, cold shower, Josh sat in his bed, frustrated as hell. He was losing his mind. All because of Sophie.

He hadn't planned on asking for her number. Actually, he had banned himself from asking for her number. But just as he was saying goodbye to her, his stupid mouth ruined his genius plan and now her number was burning through his phone.

Knowing he wouldn't be able to sleep, he was writing. Or at least trying to. His earlier anger and frustration that he had wanted to get out onto paper had disappeared.

Finally he gave in to his curiosity and picked up his phone. Sophie hadn't texted him. Not even a 'thanks for a great evening' text. And definitely not a 'come back to my room so we can ravish each other' text. He searched for her in a messenger app and saw she was online.

It was one thirty in the morning. What on earth was she still doing up?

Now his fingers turned traitor on him as he typed a message to her.

What are you still doing up? I thought you would have passed out asleep by now.

Hating his desperation, he hit the Send button. Usually he had to push women away, and now the one woman he didn't want to push away didn't want him. Maybe that was why she was so tempting and turning him into an emotional wreck? Minutes passed by like hours. Still no reply.

Huffing out his frustration, he settled himself further down in his bed, punching at the pillows to get comfortable. He needed sleep. Just a bit of sleep to come to his senses. It was probably for the best—for some reason he seemed to keep forgetting she was off limits.

As he took calming in and out breaths, counting to ten and then back again, his phone dinged.

Eyes flying open like a hawk, he pounced on his phone and the new message icon glinting at him. His heart hammered in his chest.

I can't sleep. What about you?

He didn't even wait a second before replying.

Me neither. I can't shut off yet.

He stared at the top of the app, the notification that she was writing a reply immediately making his heart beat faster. And then…nothing. She had stopped writing. Then she started again. And then nothing. Until finally a message came through.

I feel the same.

That was it? That's what had taken her all that time to write? A little inkling, or maybe it was hope, lit in his heart that perhaps she was just as conflicted about this whole situation as he was.

Wanna talk?

Unable to look at his phone anymore and wait for her reply, he threw it down and pushed the palms of his hands into his eyes. Bright lights flashed in the darkness. *Ding.*

Yes.

A smile erupted on his face and he almost gave a *whoop* of joy. Quickly hitting the video call button, he waited…again… for an eternity for her to pick up.

Shit. Sophie nibbled her lip, staring in horror at her ringing phone, Josh's profile picture glaring at her. Even the little photo of him had her body simmering all over. The red and green Decline and Accept buttons vibrated for her attention. When he'd asked her if she wanted to talk, she'd thought he just meant texting back and forth for a bit. Not a video call.

She looked down at her little pyjama vest top, her bust spilling out of it. What the hell was happening to her? Josh Heart was calling her, and she was about to answer the call looking like she did.

But there was no way she was about to reject him. So she yanked up the top a bit further to save embarrassing herself. She couldn't even think about the fact her face was now bare of make-up and her hair combed back in a ponytail. He was about to get the shock of his life.

Gulping, she held the green Accept button and waited for the connection.

Josh was sitting in his bed, a black t-shirt stretching across his pecs and tight around his biceps. "Hey." He smiled at her and the world stopped.

"Hey," she replied, nibbling her lip again. "Sorry, I look so rough. I wasn't expecting to see anyone." She tried to subtly position the phone at the most flattering angle…while giving herself some modesty…while appearing as if she wasn't doing anything. It was rather difficult, and she wasn't sure she had succeeded.

"You don't look rough at all. You're as beautiful as ever."

Her insides seemed to melt. Whoa, could he be any more of a heartthrob?

"So what's on your mind?" he asked.

"I don't know, everything really." She sighed, looking around her little room, trying to focus on something other than his beautiful face. She just couldn't concentrate when she looked at him.

"Soph?" She turned her gaze on him. "I'm here to listen. What's wrong?" He waited a heartbeat longer. "Did you dump your boyfriend?"

She gulped. Was she that obvious? "Yes."

"Good."

She couldn't help smiling at the look of joy on his face. "You're meant to tell me you're sorry, you know?" She laughed.

"I know. And I'm sorry that you're hurting. But I'm not sorry you dumped that jackass."

She laughed again. "Well, to be honest, I'm not really hurting. It was well past overdue. I just can't believe I didn't do it sooner." She relaxed against her pillow.

"That's my girl." The smile lifting the corners of his luscious lips and lighting his eyes made her all warm inside. God, he was sinfully handsome.

"Why can't you sleep?" she asked, just the tiniest bit of her wanting him to say it was because of her. She had to remind herself that celebrities like Josh Heart didn't fall for some random girl they had just met. She had obviously been reading way too many fairy tales to her students. Maybe next week she should start reading them something with a bit of action in it.

But it was Josh's turn to shrug his shoulders and avoid eye contact.

"Hey." She pouted. "That's not fair. I told you, you have to tell me."

He sighed, shrugging again. Maybe it really was because of her?

"I don't know, probably because of the award. Maybe I'm getting old and jaded."

Sophie's heart took a nosedive. Well, really? Did she really think he was tossing and turning in bed about her? Yep, she was definitely going to head to the library and pick up a book that didn't end with a happily ever after.

Suddenly not caring about the right camera angles anymore, she lay on her side and propped her phone up on a scatter cushion to free her hands. Snuggling down, she considered him. "You don't really think that, do you?" How could he not see how talented he was? "To even be nominated for one of those awards means you belong in the industry. You aren't too old, you're still releasing absolute tunes. I mean, come on."

"It's a tough business," he said, frowning. "It doesn't matter how many sold-out tours you've had, or how many number one hits you've released. It's always about what's next. And it just seems to be getting harder."

"I can't even imagine how tough it must be."

Sure, her day-to-day life of being a teacher was vastly different from Josh's, but she could sympathise. She'd never been someone who wanted to be famous—the lack of privacy, and the perception you were everyone's property and that you owed strangers everything never sat right with her. The money and freedom to do what you wanted would be great. But tonight had proved to her that celebrities didn't actually have freedom. They were always beholden to someone. But Josh had a talent. And he obviously thrived on sharing that with the world. And the world loved him for it.

"You belong here, you must know that," she said. She stifled a yawn, not wanting him to think he was boring her. He was anything but boring. Even across a video call, she was enthralled by him.

"You're tired," he stated.

"No, honestly, I'm fine."

"You look ready to fall asleep. I'll leave you."

"No, no, no," she said hurriedly, desperately not wanting him to go. If he disappeared now, she wasn't sure when she would ever see him again. "I'm fine, honestly."

He considered her for a moment, seemingly assessing whether she was lying or not. "Did you enjoy yourself tonight?" he asked, and her smile immediately broke free.

"Every second."

"You were a natural. Everyone loved you, I could tell. I must admit, award ceremonies usually aren't nearly half as much fun as tonight was."

"I don't believe you for a second. How could a massive party filled with celebrities and freebies not ever be fun?" Although Josh was smiling, something dulled in his eyes. As if someone had sprinkled dust over a diamond. "Maybe you just need to take me next time." She wasn't sure what had made her say it, but she wanted to see his sparkle come back. Thankfully it did.

"Yes, maybe." He smirked at her. "I normally leave just after the main course. I get fed up with it all."

"What, you don't even stay for dessert? I'm not sure we can be friends if that's the case," she joked easily with him.

He laughed with her, the sound filling her room and her heart. "I have the meat course and then I bolt. I could tell you were a dessert lover by the way you devoured your chocolate ganache and, what was it? Avocado ice cream?"

"Actually, it was coconut and avocado ice cream. Which,

although I was very dubious about trying it, it really worked." She raised a teasing eyebrow at him. "Sometimes you just have to try things."

"Yes," he mused, his eyes smouldering. "I'll try to remember that in future."

"Well, anyway," she said, feeling his eyes burning holes into her. "I finished yours when you went to congratulate Daniel Sampson on his award."

"Ah!" His laughter was back. "Did you now? I wondered where that had gone to. Cheeky little minx."

"Well, it was clear you weren't going to eat it, and I don't leave anything chocolate, so, sorry not sorry."

"I would've given it to you had I known you wanted it."

"Oh, I wanted it all right." She laughed, and then stopped at the look in his eyes. The tiger ready to pounce again. She bit her lip, stopping herself from saying anything else.

She had been talking about dessert, but at some point it started to sound like she was talking about wanting him. His eyes pierced hers, searching for something. Thank God he was on the other end of the phone, otherwise she might have jumped into his arms there and then.

Josh felt himself harden at her words. *I wanted it all right.* He knew she was talking about dessert, but maybe, just maybe, a part of her was talking about wanting him too. They were in dangerous territory and he knew it. He was playing with fire, breaking all of his rules. They needed to get back on safer ground.

"I'll remember in future to always give you my dessert." *Shit.* That wasn't really any better, now he was practically promising to take her out.

Sophie scrunched her perfect little lips together. "Good." She took a deep breath. "Your team seems lovely."

He was grateful she had chosen a safe topic. They spoke for a little while longer about his team and the night, Josh desperately trying to ignore his bulge, which was nigh on impossible with Sophie's breasts practically spilling out of her tank top as she lay down.

An hour into their video call, where they discussed everything and nothing at the same time, he excused himself to visit the bathroom, hoping that a bit of distance would settle him down and give him relief from his throbbing groin. He was unsuccessful.

When he returned shortly after to his bed and his phone, he apologised to Sophie. "Sorry about that." He looked at the phone once he was settled in bed, his hard-on out of shot. All he saw was a black screen. "Sophie?" he called out. Maybe she had gone to the toilet too? He gave her a couple of minutes. "Sophie?" he called out again and listened. Nothing. The screen was still blank but the call was connected. What had happened?

A crazy thought popped into his head. Was she okay? *Shit.* What if she wasn't? Surely she had just fallen asleep while she waited for him?

But then again, surely her phone would still show her sleeping. After all, she had propped it up. He called for her again, louder this time. She hadn't looked overly sleepy. Yes, it was now almost three o'clock in the morning, but if she was sleeping she'd hear him shouting through the phone.

He tried again, panic seizing his body. What if something had happened to her? Could she be hurt? Could someone have hurt her?

No. He scoffed at his preposterous idea. That wouldn't have happened. She would have merely fallen asleep. He tried calling her name again.

But what if her stupid ex-boyfriend had been so pissed off that he'd come and hurt her?

Without another thought, he bolted out of his bed, grabbed his phone and room key and flew down the hallway, not even stopping to put his shoes on. That arsehole better not have hurt her. He would be dead if he did.

CHAPTER 7

Bang, bang, bang.

Thudding sounded around her, growing louder and more incessant. God, that was really annoying. Just go down to the front desk and ask for a spare room key. *Arsehole.*

Shoving her head under her pillow, Sophie tried to drown out the noise.

"Sophie?"

She jolted upright in bed. *Fuck,* the banging was on her door. She went to the door as quickly as she could to stop the god-awful noise.

Just as she was unlatching it, the shouting sounded again. "Sophie?"

"Shush." She yanked her door open. A distraught Josh Heart stood in front of her, his hand poised to bang again. "What are you doing here?" she whispered loudly.

Relief washed across his face. And then that relief morphed into something dark and brooding. His eyes filled with desire, and he pulled her to him and kissed her, right on the lips, his mouth squashed against hers in desperation. Then his tongue forced its way into her mouth and lapped at hers.

She groaned into him, welcoming his warm, hard body pushed against hers, but he tightened his grip on her arms and pushed her free of him.

"Fuck," he whispered, his breath so close it blew over her. "Are you okay?" His eyes left hers and searched behind her.

"Huh?" she replied in her sleepy, lusty state. What was happening here? Had he really just kissed her?

"I was so worried about you. Are you hurt? Are you okay?"

"What? No." Panic lit his face, and she clarified, "I mean yes I'm okay, and no I'm not hurt." She shook her head, trying to get some coherent thought back. "What's going on?"

"So no one is with you? You're not hurt in any way?" His eyes searched hers.

"What's going on, Josh? You're confusing me."

"I came back to the phone and it was black, you had gone, and I was shouting your name but you didn't respond. I was worried about you. I thought maybe your arsehole ex-boyfriend had shown up and hurt you."

"Huh?" Her sleepy brain couldn't understand what was happening. "Josh, no one is here apart from you. I obviously just fell asleep and didn't hear you."

"You're sure no one is here?"

Knowing that he wouldn't settle until he saw the truth for himself, she stepped to the side and let him through. He barged past, knocking into the door frame, a man on a mission to find an imaginary intruder.

"No one is here!" she tried to tell him again, but he was intent on searching her bathroom and then under the bed, in the wardrobe and behind the curtains. "Look!" She pointed to the bed. "My phone has fallen from the cushion and is face down. I must have been in a deep sleep and not heard you." She grabbed his hand as he was still looking around, his lips pursed, his once slicked-back hair now tousled. "Josh," she whispered, pulling him to her. "I'm fine, I promise." His hard body felt heavenly against hers.

Knowing only one thing that would break his search off, she pulled his head down to hers. Rising on her tiptoes, she wound her arm around his neck and brushed her nose against his, testing to see if he would pull away from her. Josh's eyes were dark, his breathing heavy, but he didn't pull away. Instead he brushed her nose back. And feeling just a bit braver, she kissed him. His eyes opened wide for a moment, before closing and then he groaned. He seemed to melt into her, his hands snaking around her body, touching every inch, every curve.

She ran her fingers through his long hair as he cupped her bum and their lips nipped at each other. Eventually she pulled away from him, taking his bottom lip gently in her teeth and pulling back before letting go.

His breath caught. "You worried me." He nuzzled her nose softly, desire lighting his eyes.

"You worried yourself," she whispered, sliding back down off her tippy toes, feeling every ridge of his incredibly hard body against hers as she did so.

He nuzzled into her neck, his deep breath sending shivers down her spine, his soft black hair tickling her cheek.

"Tell me what you want." He whispered it so quietly that she wasn't sure he had even said it.

"You," she breathed back.

At that, he grabbed her bum once more, hoisted her up so she could wrap her legs around his hips, and threw her down on the bed. She let out a moan of desire as he kissed his way down her neck and her bare chest, tiny shivers erupting all over her as he went, while she tried to catch her breath.

He stopped at her breasts and lifted his gaze to stare into her eyes. "I've been wanting to do this ever since I first laid eyes on you." And then he ripped her vest top right down the middle, exposing her breasts.

She moaned with desire again, breathing fast, and he bent down to devour her nipples. She had never been so turned on in all her life.

Rearing up again, his eyes full of promise, Josh yanked her little, pink pyjama shorts from her, leaving her naked before him.

"Absolutely perfect," he moaned, diving between her legs and nipping at her. Pushing his tongue between her folds, he licked and sucked and teased her, quickly bringing her to climax, the fastest she had ever come.

Before she could even catch her breath, he dragged his t-shirt off and threw it on the floor, then pulled down his boxers and jogging bottoms in one, his erection springing free. Glorious. He pounced back on her, kissing her roughly with need. She wrapped her legs around him, using her heels to bring him closer to her entrance.

And then, just as he was about to enter her, he exclaimed, "Fuck!"

"What?" She moved beneath him, desperate to feel him slide inside her despite having just come.

"I don't have a condom." He sighed, screwing up his face in frustration.

"Wait here." She freed herself from his body and ran naked into the bathroom.

Josh waited, a tug of jealousy pulling on his heart. If Sophie did have a condom, it was meant for her ex-boyfriend. Thinking of her with another man made his skin prickle.

She returned, triumphantly holding a foil packet in front of her. She tried to cover up her body as she went, one arm crossed over her full breasts, and the other the glorious sight between her legs.

As she neared the bed, Josh grabbed her by the hand and rolled her over him. "Don't you dare cover your body in front of me," he whispered in her ear.

Locking her eyes onto his, she moved her arms from her breasts, exposing herself to him.

"You're the most beautiful woman I have ever seen." He watched an internal war rage in her eyes.

Taking a gulp, she finally responded. "You're not too bad yourself." She ripped open the condom wrapper with her teeth and scooted down his body, touching his abs and hips as she went, scraping his skin with her fingernails. As she grazed his body, she rubbed across his rod, letting it caress her. He stifled a groan. The wanton look in her eye almost made him release.

He watched as she licked him from base to tip. If she carried on much longer, he wouldn't last. When he moaned her name, she responded to him and took him into her mouth, sliding up and down him excruciatingly slowly.

He closed his eyes, allowing the bliss to travel all over his body. A brief moment of cold air brought him to open his eyes, and he saw Sophie roll the condom down onto him. He let her finish and then hoisted her up again as if she were a doll, and placed her straddled across his hips.

"Tell me what you want," she asked, using his words against him. She was pure fire. Pure danger. He was going to get burnt. But he just couldn't help himself. He could die happy once he'd been with her.

"Touch yourself," he ordered her, and to his delight she obeyed him and caressed her breasts and nipples. Without any further orders, she lowered her fingers to her clitoris and rubbed herself on top of him, her eyes closing in her own pleasure. She was a goddess.

"Tell me what you want," she groaned again, still playing with herself.

He could have lain there all day watching her, but the opportunity to have her could not be passed up. "Take me," he demanded.

"I need more." She rocked into her fingers.

"Take me and sink yourself onto me. Slowly. Inch by inch. I want to feel you slide down onto me. I want to feel you stretch for me. Fuck me, Sophie."

She did as she was told, at such a pace that he had to fight his desire to buck into her. Trying to savour every moment, he guided her hips down as she continued playing with herself. He was bewitched. She rocked back and forth on him, lost in her ecstasy, her moaning getting louder, her hips starting to buck wildly.

He held on to her hips, guiding her, keeping their rhythm. Slamming into her harder, he could feel her pleasure building, needing to be released again. Instead of giving into her, he slowed their pace once more and rotated his hips around and around, enticing her further.

She dropped her hands from her body to either side of his head and he met her lips, kissing her tenderly. Their pace slowed together, teasing each other. Loving each other. Until there was nothing more for it, but to come apart at the seams together. Sophie called out his name, throwing her head back and stilling, and he quickly followed.

She nuzzled into his neck, trying to gain control of her breathing once more, and he traced lazy circles across her back and arms. They stayed like that for a while, not talking, just being, until they fell asleep, naked in each other's arms. Safe from the world outside. Safe from their future.

CHAPTER 8

Sophie stirred from her sleep, desperate to feel that hard body again. She felt around in bed looking for Josh, wanting to wrap her arms around him and nuzzle into his neck.

The other side of the bed was empty.

She opened her eyes. Josh was nowhere to be seen. Stretching in bed, she listened for him in the bathroom. Nothing.

Had he left? She sat up in bed, looking for his clothes. They were gone.

He couldn't have left. Surely not. She pulled on a top and trousers, suddenly feeling dirty and used. She'd never had a one-night stand before…but she hadn't thought this was a one-night stand. She hadn't thought at all.

Checking her phone, hoping he had texted her at least, her heart plummeted. Nothing.

He couldn't have just left her. People didn't do that, did they? Surely he had the balls to tell her it was just one night, and it meant nothing to him? She rubbed her eyes, willing the tears in them not to fall, her throat burning. She was more upset about this than she was about breaking up with Scott.

Maybe he'd just gone to get them a coffee. That's what happened in movies, right? The woman woke up panicking, and then the man came back in with a coffee. Yes, that must be what was going to happen. Josh Heart was a celebrity, but he seemed like such a nice guy. A nice guy wouldn't just leave.

Needing to distract herself, she ran a shower and packed her bags ready to check out. Her muscles ached with exhaustion from only getting a couple of hours of sleep last night.

By the time she had showered and dressed, it was clear Josh wasn't returning. Sighing, she checked around the room one last time for any bits she had forgotten. Her phone rang. Belle. Not wanting to go over the whole night with her friend in minute detail just yet, she silenced her phone and shoved it into the bottom of her bag.

She closed the door to her hotel room—on the perfect night that she would never experience again—and rode the lift down to check out.

As she left the hotel, she noticed a gaggle of people congregating and jostling at the hotel doors. Probably there to see some of the celebrities leaving this morning after the award ceremony.

The doorman held the door open for her, an apologetic look on his face. She smiled and thanked him and then was hit by the flashing of cameras, the noise of people firing questions, and was jostled along in the throng.

What on earth was going on? She picked up her pace, hoping to escape the crowd before whatever celebrity came out of the doors behind her. But as she moved, so did the crowd. And as she pulled her overnight suitcase with her, phones and cameras and voice recorders were shoved in her face.

She was surrounded on all sides by people she didn't know. As she moved quickly along, so did they.

"Sorry, I'm just trying to get through!" she called out to the crowd, hoping they would make way. "Excuse me, please. I can't see where I'm going."

Then she heard it. Her name.

Amongst all the calling, people were shouting her name and asking her questions. What on earth was happening? How did all of these people know who she was? She kept her head down and moved as quickly as she could, tripping over the people in front and trying to push her way through. There was no let up.

"Sophie, how was last night?"

"Sophie, how was your first time on the red carpet?"

"Sophie, what do you do for a living? Will we be seeing you again?"

"Sophie, are you in a relationship with Josh Heart?"

"Sophie, what's it like to be dating the UK's most eligible bachelor?"

"Sophie, is it true you two spent the night together?"

Sophie blanched. Were these paparazzi? What should she do? How did they know all of this? She walked as quickly as she was able to, along the busy London road to the tube station. The paparazzi and journalists never relented. They kept pace with her every step, taking pictures of her, trying to get her to respond.

All she could do was duck her head and try to run for her life.

Josh was a coward.

There was no denying it. He couldn't ever remember leaving a woman after spending the night with her. Despite his playboy image, if he was with a woman, he was serious about her—they were exclusive. He didn't do one-night stands. And he certainly didn't do one-night stands with fans.

He pushed the buttons on the treadmill in his newly refurbished home gym to run faster, needing to work out the tension in his body, the dread that had settled in his stomach and the tight ropes around his heart.

When he'd got home that morning—the smell of fresh paint and sawn wood filling his luxurious London home— he'd tried writing lyrics, tried composing, tried singing. But nothing helped. They were his usual go-to coping mechanisms, but they just weren't working. He couldn't concentrate. He couldn't think properly. So now, he was running. Running away from Sophie. Running to forget Sophie.

They had spent one perfect evening together, one perfect night in bed. It should have been enough. But right now, it wasn't. He had broken every rule in his book for her. He had those rules for a reason, and last night he had lost all his senses to her.

Sure, Sophie didn't seem like a super-fan who would lose her head over him like Emily had. But it was a risk he hadn't wanted to take. And now he had jeopardised her, just like he had Emily.

This had to be better for Sophie, hadn't it? Yes, she would probably have woken up this morning pissed off that he'd left, but it was better for her to be hurt now than to lose her head later down the line. He didn't want to be responsible for another life, and when it came to fans, they were so enamoured and wrapped up in the life of celebrities and the fairy tale of being with them that they lost all sense of themselves. Sophie didn't deserve that. That's why he had rules. That's why he didn't fuck fans.

Emily had started off just like Sophie—a brief encounter where they had clicked, Emily dazzled by her celebrity crush and Josh enamoured with her happy-go-lucky nature. But after a short time, things started to change. Emily grew less easy-going, more erratic and demanding, wanting to spend time at all the parties he was invited to, schmoozing with other celebrities and flirting outrageously with them, demanding they ate at fancy restaurants and holidayed in exclusive resorts.

Six months into their relationship, Emily no longer resembled the woman he fell for. She had morphed into someone he hated—highly strung, materialistic and demanding. She wasn't with him because she loved him. It was the fame, the money and the power that she was after. And before he realised it, she was into the drug scene, and there was no going back.

He shook his head, trying to clear the memories. Memories he'd tried to put behind him years ago. He couldn't bear that happening to Sophie. This life was a poison, and he needed to protect her from it.

A call on his mobile broke through the music playing for his workout. His publicist, probably after some feedback from last night. Sighing, he cut her call off and slowed the treadmill, ready to lift some weights.

Towelling off his sweaty forehead, he guzzled his water and moved shaky-legged to the weights. He was pushing hard today, but he needed to, to forget.

Another call came through, interrupting his playlist again. He looked down and froze when he saw Sophie's name on the caller ID.

Fuck.

His fingers hovered over the button. She deserved an explanation, she deserved the time to yell and scream at him, call him all the names under the sun. As he stared at the screen, questioning if he should answer or not, he waited too long and the call ended. *What a fucking coward.*

He slumped on the bench, staring at his reflection in the mirrors, despising himself.

His phone *dinged* and he saw the voicemail icon appear. Lifting the phone to his ear, he listened with bated breath.

"Hi Josh, this is Sophie. As much as I want to rip you to shreds right now, I have bigger fish to fry. I was just ambushed by journalists and paparazzi outside the hotel, screaming at me, asking me questions about you and about us spending the night together. I have no idea how they know. I don't want that life, Josh. How do I get them to go away? It was the scariest thing that's ever happened to me. And what's going to happen to my job? If this makes the magazines, the parents of my pupils and the leadership team at school are going to go mental. I could lose my job over this, Josh." She paused, taking a deep breath before continuing. "Anyway, I didn't expect you to answer or to care that my life could be ruined. If you cared, you wouldn't have left without a word. Thanks for nothing, Josh." She took a shuddering breath. "I wish I'd never met you."

And the voicemail was over.

CHAPTER 9

As if today wasn't bad enough already, the inevitable call came through. Sophie sighed, despising how quickly her world had turned upside down.

She answered the call. "Scott, I told you not to call me." Slumping onto her sofa, she pulled her dressing gown around her. She had been home for about an hour now, shielding calls from everyone on her contact list and loads more from people who weren't. She had shut her curtains, blocking out the bright sunshine and any more sneaky people with cameras.

"That was before you cheated on me!" he yelled down the phone. He always did have a bit of a temper.

"I have never cheated on you." She pulled her legs up to her chest.

"How do you explain all these headlines and photos then?" he countered.

"You can't believe what you see in the papers. Paparazzi are literally paid to follow celebrities around, photographing their every movement, trying to make something out of nothing. I didn't cheat on you." She chewed her lip. Technically she hadn't, but he would still be hurt to know that she'd spent the night with someone else the same night she broke up with him.

"Did you dump me so you could be with him?" he asked.

"No, Scott. I dumped you because I was finally done with how you've treated me over the years, and because I finally realised it would never get better. Look…" She rubbed her temple. "I know you want to find a reason as to why I left you that isn't because of you, but there isn't one."

"So you aren't with anyone?" Scott's breathing was steadier and at least he wasn't yelling anymore.

"No. I'm single." There was silence on the other end of the phone. "Is that everything, Scott? Are you feeling better?"

"Yep."

"Great." He hung up on her. "I'm glad someone is," she said to herself, throwing her phone on the sofa.

Sophie slammed her car door shut as hard as she could on Monday afternoon, willing all of her pain and anguish to vanish into the door. Her heart thumped and her hands shook as she gripped the steering wheel. It hadn't helped one bit.

Twisting the ignition on, she blew out her breath. She would not give anyone the satisfaction of seeing her sitting in the staff car park crying.

There had been no avoiding how horrible today would be. But the reality had been worse than she'd expected. She needed her brother, John. He'd know what to say to help her feel better.

She drove through her home village of Winton Green to his pub, The Dog. Well, technically it was Tony who owned the pub, and John worked the bar. But Tony had been like a brother to her in the five or six years they had known each other, so, same difference.

She tapped her steering wheel with her fingers as she drove, needing a distraction from the thoughts in her head. Golden fields flashed past her windows on her short drive, the Kentish country roads almost empty.

She sighed. How had she ended up here, her world in complete disarray? On Friday, she had left work next in line for the associate headteacher role, one she had been working towards since leaving university. She had her students' trust and their parents' respect. And she had a boyfriend, albeit a crappy one. Now, she had no boyfriend, the parents at school were all whispering about her, throwing looks of judgement her way, and she was pretty sure her 'antics', as her boss had called them, had jeopardised her promotion, too. Her thirties were turning into a disaster.

She turned this way and that down the country lanes to the pub from memory. Winton Green had always been her home, apart from a few years that she had spent away at university. She had loved coming back home to work at the primary school she'd attended as a child, feeling like a member of the community. Now she hated it. It was harder to escape the knowing looks of everyone she knew than it had been shaking off the paparazzi.

She pulled up at the pub, which overlooked the quaint village green. Striding towards the open pub door, she stopped, listening to the chatter inside. It sounded busy.

She chewed her cheek. This village was her home, the place she belonged. Yet now, listening to the murmur of people drinking inside, a cold sweat of dread trickled down her spine. She couldn't go in there. Everyone would look at her again. Judge her. Whisper about her.

She backed away. Away from the support her brother would give her. Away from the people she had grown up with.

As she fumbled with her car keys, her eyes filling with tears, she felt a wet dog nose touch her arm. Max, the beautiful, chocolate-brown spaniel that belonged to Tony, nudged her again. She looked up. Wherever Max was, Tony was sure to be.

Tony and his girlfriend Jodie walked out of their cottage just next to the pub, smiling bright, genuine smiles at her. She had never seen Tony as happy as he was when he was with Jodie. They had recently moved in with each other after falling in love while Jodie decorated his cottage. Jodie was busy building up a successful interior design company she had started from scratch when she moved to Winton Green.

"Hey, Soph," Tony called to her. "You just leaving?" He nodded back to the pub, his pride and joy.

"Erm." Sophie scratched Max's tufty head to calm herself. "I didn't make it in, actually."

"Oh, really?" Tony and Jodie stopped when they reached her. Tony's face was screwed up in confusion, and he scratched at the dark stubble on his chin.

Jodie rolled her eyes at him and went over to Sophie, wrapping her arms around her without saying a word, pulling her in for a tight hug. Sophie sighed and soaked in the comfort from her new friend.

"Are you okay?" Jodie eventually asked, pulling away, her deep-brown, curly hair being swept by the breeze.

Sophie mumbled, not wanting to cry. "I wanted to speak to John…but I just can't."

"I'll grab him for you." Jodie rubbed her arm and made a move to go into the pub.

"No, it's fine," Sophie called. "Honestly, I have lots of lesson plans to do and I'm getting a headache. I'm just going to go home."

"You sure? You know he'd want to be there for you," Tony said, finally cottoning on.

"Yeah." She brushed them off. "Honestly, it's nothing." She turned to go.

"Soph?" Tony called out. She turned to face him, dreading what he had to say. "Come over for dinner one night this week, yeah?" Worry knitted his brows.

"Course," she called back to him with a wave, hoping her fake, blasé attitude would fool them both.

Tony linked his hand with Jodie's and pulled her close, while Sophie turned to get in her car and away from their happiness that stabbed at her like daggers.

"Josh?" The echo sounded across the marble floor. "Whereabouts are you, mate?"

Josh sighed. Maybe he shouldn't have given Sean a key to his house. Every day for a whole week, Sean had let himself into Josh's home to check up on him.

"Up here!" he called back, and waited for Sean's head to appear around the door frame of his music studio.

"Hiya!" Sean's smile lit up the room, showing his straight white teeth.

"Seriously?" Josh raised an eyebrow at him. "Do you really need to come over every day to check in on me? I told you, I'm fine." He pushed away from the piano on his wheeled chair and grabbed them both a bottle of water from his mini fridge.

"And I told you, I don't believe you." Sean caught the bottle Josh threw to him and went to inspect the notes on the piano. Josh let him—it was no use hiding it, Sean had already seen what he'd been writing this week. "And until you stop writing stuff like this"—Sean pointed to the papers—"I'll know you aren't alright."

Josh shook his head and turned his back, fiddling with a

record player to put some music on. "You don't know what you're talking about," he muttered.

"Josh, I've known you since school. I've read or listened to most of your music, and that…that stuff tells me more than you can say."

"I didn't think you liked listening to my music?" Josh sat in the black leather armchair across from Sean.

"I listen to it when you release a song, so I know what everyone else is listening to, and that's it. I prefer my music more…" He clicked his fingers, searching for the words.

"Drum and bassy?"

Sean clicked and pointed at his friend, relaxing back on the sofa. "Yeah, that's the one. But you're very popular. I can't avoid your bloody music."

"It's always nice to know my number-one friend is my number-one fan." Josh shook his head, laughing, and kicked his feet up on the coffee table.

"Have you been out today?"

"Nope," Josh replied, swiping his thumb over a button in the arm of his chair. From the corner of his eye, he could see Sean shaking his head.

"That's it then, I'm taking you out." He slapped his thighs, put his bottle of water on the table and stood up.

"What?" Josh followed him out of the studio. "What do you mean you're taking me out?" Come to think of it, Sean did look like he'd prepared to go out. He was wearing a dark blue dress shirt rolled up at the sleeves and he'd been a bit too heavy-handed with his aftershave.

"You haven't been out of the house for a week." Sean strode across the hallway and Josh went after him.

"So?"

"So…you're hiding. But you don't need to hide. Fresh air and a change of scene will do that mind of yours good." Sean walked into Josh's master bedroom and surveyed the scene, shaking his head. "Come on, man, how can you even begin to tell me you're alright?" He raised his hand at the bombsite before him.

Josh normally kept an immaculate household—everything had its place and the sleek lines of his minimalist furniture were not normally spoiled by anything that shouldn't be there. But right now, at that very moment—well, for a whole week, really—he hadn't been his usual obsessive self. His normally clear side tables were piled high with clothes, his bed was unmade and the towel from his shower that morning was still on the floor.

"I just couldn't be arsed today." He shrugged, looking down at his bare feet.

"This doesn't look like you could be arsed for a whole week. Coincidentally, isn't that when you last saw Sophie?" His friend raised one eyebrow at him, a slight smile at the corner of his lips.

Josh couldn't help but wince at her name. Every time he thought about her or heard her name, his belly did a flip before his heart sank. He couldn't believe how he'd treated her. He'd never treated anyone like that before, and the one person who'd resonated with his very soul was the one person he'd hurt the most.

Sean nudged him into his en-suite. "Take a shower, chuck on some nice clothes. I've got a place in mind where I don't think you'll be recognised."

Sean closed the door in Josh's face before he could argue. Looked like he was going out.

~

"Take those bloody sunglasses off!" Belle ripped the dark glasses off Sophie's face. "What? You really think anyone is going to come over and say anything to you?" She raised her eyebrow and sipped her glass of wine.

"No, of course they won't. They'll just say it all behind my back!" Sophie ducked her head as best she could.

They were sitting in the corner of The Dog. Belle had forced her to get out even though Sophie had tried to make excuses.

"Soph, you're going to have to move on from all of this, lovely. Come on now, you're old news."

"Yes, I'm old news to the magazines. But not to the parents at school, the PTA, the governors or the headmistress."

She had endured a week of hell. Her boss had warned her that she needed to behave with self-respect and decorum, that her actions reflected on the school and could jeopardise her chance of becoming an associate headteacher. She had promised that nothing like this would ever happen again, but she could still feel the eyes on the back of her head, watching every move she made. The only thing that had saved her week were her students. They always made her feel better, and thankfully they were young enough to not know anything that was going on.

Sophie stirred her drink with her straw. The shifty looks she got from every member of staff and every parent was hurtful. But what stung more was the radio silence from Josh. He had never returned her call.

What he had done, though, was release a statement to 'clarify' the situation, stating that he'd acted as any gentleman would that night by walking her back to her hotel room after the award ceremony, and that nothing else had happened between them. But in the eyes of every Tom, Dick and Harry, it just cemented the speculation that they had spent the night together.

Which they had…but that wasn't the point.

"Come on Sophie, you didn't lose your job. You're on your

best behaviour and they would be stupid to pass you over again for the associate head role. Just keep your chin up, your face out of the papers, and this will all blow over." Belle had started to get snappy with Sophie every time they spoke about it.

"I know." Sophie nodded her head, trying to convince herself as well. "I just can't believe I fell for another idiot. I just seem to pick losers."

"Well…" Belle tucked her long, dark hair behind her ear. "Scott was a total loser. But Josh was just a one-night thing. Yes, he's turned out to be a bit of an idiot, but it's hardly a track record, is it?" Sophie chewed her lip. "Sophie, please tell me you don't think that's a track record?" Belle's shoulders shrank, all life seeming to leave her body.

"Well, I haven't ever picked anyone good, have I?"

Belle banged her head on the table and let out a wail. "Sophie, it's two guys! Do you even know how many idiots I've dated? How many one-night stands I thought were a good idea and would lead me to a happily ever after? Yet here I am, still alone, still single. You've spent all your adult life with Scott, which yes, you know I think was a complete waste of time. But him and a one-night stand are not a track record."

Sophie shrugged, still not seeing it any other way. "I just don't want to turn out like my mother," she said, wincing.

Belle's jaw dropped, her eyebrows drawing together. "Sophie," she whispered, grasping onto her friend's hand. "Please listen to me when I say this." She stared into Sophie's eyes. "You couldn't be any more different to your mum. I promise you. You two, when it comes to men, are poles apart." She squeezed her hand tight. "Please don't tell me you stuck with sucky Scott because you didn't want to turn out like your mum?"

Sophie shrugged. Belle had hit the nail on the head. For years she had tried to make her relationship work with Scott, not wanting to throw it down the drain and move on to another guy, just like her mum had over the years. She couldn't remember a time when her mum was just her mum, single and happy. When her dad left before she could even form a memory of him, Sophie's mum had hopped from one man to the next, searching for the missing piece in her life. The only constant Sophie'd had was her big brother, John.

"Come on, I'm getting you a Jägerbomb." Belle slapped the table and went up to the bar where John was waiting. Sophie didn't even have time to argue that it was one o'clock on a Sunday afternoon.

She sat silently, looking around the pub. No one was staring at her. Maybe she was being paranoid. Maybe no one here actually cared. Finally she let out the breath she was holding. She was safe here. John wouldn't let anything happen to her, and nor would Belle. These were her people, her entourage. And for the first time in weeks, she let herself smile.

"And what do you think you're doing here?"

Sophie heard the shouting and twisted to see Belle glaring towards the door. The chatter in the pub had died down and everyone's attention was on Belle. Sophie's jaw dropped when she saw who her friend's anger was aimed at.

For a moment, fear pinned her to her seat, and then, steadily, she rose from her chair and made her way over to tame her friend.

"I literally cannot believe the audacity you have to step foot in this place." Belle stamped her foot like an insolent child. Her temper always simmered close to the edge, just waiting to erupt.

Sophie watched as James, the local vet, who happened to be Belle's brother's best friend, stepped towards Belle. Holding onto her forearm, he lowered his head and spoke so quietly that Sophie couldn't hear what he was saying.

"No, I will not calm down." Belle wrenched her arm from James and pointed at the newcomers. "Not until they leave!" Sophie stopped her slow, torturous walk just at the edge of the commotion. The people around her seemed to be turning their attention away. "John, bar them, chuck them out."

John scoffed in bewilderment. "Belle, I don't even know who these guys are!"

"You're kidding me. That 'guy'"—Belle made air quotes—"is the one who's ruined your sister's life!"

John turned to him, his face as hard as stone, his jaw clenching. Sophie saw the recognition light his eyes as he took in Josh, still standing in the doorway. Josh was frozen to the spot, staring at Sophie, a strange look on his face.

"That may be the case," John finally said. "But he hasn't done anything wrong here, and I can't just chuck him out." He looked to Sophie, an apology written all over his face. Not that he needed to apologise. She got it.

Belle, however…did not. "What?" she exclaimed, her arms flailing wildly before coming down to slap her thighs.

James stepped up to Belle again, blocking her view of Josh with his bright-white shirt and large body. He brushed the hair away from her face and tucked it behind her ear, then lifted her chin to make sure she looked at him. Her breath hitched, and the air vibrated between the two of them. Holy hell. Was he going to kiss her?

"Belle?" he whispered, searching her eyes.

"But…" she tried to argue.

"Belle," he said calmly again. "Come with me." And he steered her away from the drama, his hand on her hip.

John spoke again, looking at Josh. "I suggest that if you're staying here, you have an apology to give and some explaining to do before you order a drink." He nodded towards Sophie.

～

The look on Sophie's face told Josh everything. Her eyebrows were drawn together, her lips were slightly parted and her eyes were full of hurt and shock.

Every look at her broke his heart.

And he had caused it all.

He had no idea who the woman was who'd started shouting at him when he and Sean entered the pub. Normally when people recognised him, they got all flustered, asking for his autograph and a selfie, wanting to talk to him and stay by his side. But when she'd recognised him, her anger had spilled out. Obviously, not everyone was a fan—it didn't matter how many number-one hits you had or world tours you'd sold out, there were still people on the planet who didn't like you or your music. But no one had ever shouted at him before.

And then when he'd seen Sophie standing just past the shouting woman, he'd understood.

"Shit," Sean whispered out the side of his mouth. "Sorry, mate." He slapped him on the back, then left him in the doorway and walked over to the tattooed barman, who apparently was Sophie's brother. Could you get any more messed up? "Don't suppose I'm all right to get a drink?"

What a traitor. If Josh had known they'd bump into Sophie, he would never have agreed to come.

"Sophie." He stepped towards her.

She stepped back, her eyes widening.

"Please, Sophie, let me talk to you." He should turn around and walk out, but he just couldn't.

Her eyes found her brother. And after a brief moment, she pulled her shoulders back, gave the smallest of nods and followed Josh out of the pub into the warming sunshine outside.

The village of Winton Green was quietly bustling for a Sunday afternoon. The summer flowers were in bloom, and the chatter and laughter from within the pub floated out onto the green. In any other circumstances, Josh would have lapped up the small community vibe, relished the anonymity that came from being in the countryside. But that had all flown out the window. When Sean had suggested they go so far out from London to find some peace, Josh had been quietly hopeful they might actually find it. How wrong could he be?

Turning round, Josh stuck his hands in his pockets and hunched his shoulders up to his ears. What on earth could he say? "I'm sorry, Sophie. If I'd known you would be here, I wouldn't have come."

She let out a small puff of air and rolled her eyes. "So, you didn't come to find me to apologise?" She searched the village green, seeming to try to find something to focus on other than him.

"I had no way of knowing you would be here." He shuffled his boot on the ground. "Sean suggested getting out and mentioned this place, as I probably wouldn't be recognised here." Josh wasn't a bad man. He'd had no intention of hurting Sophie—he wouldn't normally just up and leave someone after spending a night together. But it was what he had needed to do to protect her. Since meeting her everything seemed to be turning on its head. He'd been an arse and he needed to apologise. And then he needed to leave. Immediately. His hands were already twitchy and wanted to take hold of her.

She closed her eyes and waited. "Well, you certainly never disappoint, do you, Josh?" Her voice was hard and cutting.

He winced. Man, she was pissed.

She carried on, anger simmering in her voice. "Here I was, thinking you had found me to apologise for the past week, and yet all I get is some 'sorry I turned up to not say sorry' shit. God…I literally have no idea how I thought you were a good guy."

She turned to leave and Josh couldn't help but instinctively grab her wrist.

"Sophie, I'm sorry for all of that. I was trying to shut you out to avoid this." He swiped his hands between the two of them. "Sophie." He waited till she looked at him. "I'm sorry."

She had to see he was a good guy really. If he could go back in time and act differently he would. But that morning, when he'd woken up next to her—her body so warm and soft, calling out to him—he had freaked out. In a flash he'd wanted more of her, more with her. But she was off limits. She had to be. And not knowing what else to do, he bolted.

"It's fine." She pulled her cardigan tight around her. "Well, it's not fine, but I accept your apology." She let out a long sigh, her shoulders seeming to deflate.

"I shouldn't have left you to the wolves. I know what the media can be like. I hoped that statement would put things right, but it just fuelled the fire."

She said nothing.

Needing to fill the void of silence, he finally admitted, "I'm a coward."

She huffed and shook her long blonde hair. "Yes, you are."

"And I know an apology doesn't make it better."

"No, it doesn't." Then, slapping her hands against her thighs, she looked at him with a tiny smile. "I will let my brother know that you can have a drink now."

He'd made progress. It wasn't perfect. She probably still hated him. But at least he'd said his piece. And hopefully that was enough to help her heal and move on.

He followed her into the pub, ignoring the sway of her hips in her miniskirt. As much as he wanted to pull her back and hold her, to feel her body melt against his, he knew if he gave in again she would get hurt. And that was something he couldn't bear.

"He can have a drink, John." Sophie waved behind her, not looking back at him, as she walked back to her friend and the man in the white shirt with rolled-up sleeves.

CHAPTER 11

"Did you apologise?" The barman narrowed his eyes and crossed his arms over his chest.

"I did, not that it makes it any better." Josh turned to see Sophie, her back towards him and her friend glaring at him. Sighing, he turned back and said, "I didn't mean to hurt her. I fucked this whole thing up."

Sean thumped him roughly on the back as if trying to stop him from choking on a bit of food. "Josh is a good man. Normally, anyway," Sean said in his defence. "Something about your sister has got him totally screwed up."

Josh threw him a scathing look. What on earth was wrong with him?

"What?" Sean asked, genuinely bewildered.

"Shut up." Josh raised his eyebrows in warning, his lips pursed.

"What?" Sean scrunched his face up. "I'm just explaining—"

"Yes. To Sophie's brother, who could easily throw us out of here and I'm sure would quite happily deck me right now. So shut up and take your drink to the corner."

Before Josh could usher Sean away from the bar, John cut

in. "To be honest," he said, a wicked smirk appearing on his face as he wiped down a glass with the tea towel hanging from his shoulder, "I'm enjoying seeing you squirm. Call it a bit of payback." He nodded to Sean to continue.

"Well, John, I've never seen him so out of sorts!"

Josh groaned. Sean had always loved a good chat with a barman.

"He's been different this past week," Sean carried on. "Moping around the place, not wanting to write…"

"I am writing."

"Not your usual shit."

"What shit is he writing now then?" John asked, obviously enjoying every second of torture Josh was experiencing.

"I don't know, I couldn't understand it. Something about losing something he never had. And then it clicked. It's about—"

"Sophie!" John said, his teeth showing behind his smile.
Sean nodded.

"It is not about Sophie," Josh insisted. "It's just a load of thoughts about stuff completely unrelated to Sophie." He gulped down his beer, commanding his shaking hand to be still.

"What about Sophie?" That shrill voice sounded again. The one that turned his insides to ice.

"Belle," Sophie called to her friend, coming over and tugging at her arm.

"No, they're talking about you and I want to know what he's got to say." Belle stood her ground, hands on her hips, foot tapping.

Josh opened his mouth to respond.

"We were just talking about the song Josh is writing about Sophie," John cut in, and placed another pint on the bar for him.

What on earth was happening here? This was the strangest encounter he had ever experienced.

For the hundredth time, he tried to explain. "It's not about Sophie." He didn't dare look at her. "It isn't anything. It's just words strung together that have no meaning." Over the past few days, he'd finally been able to start writing, finally breaking through his writer's block. And now he was regretting it. Right at this second, it would be better if he were still suffering from insomnia, still unable to find the words to put pen to paper, and still unable to mix those words with music.

"Sing it to us then," the beastly Belle demanded.

Spluttering the beer he had been sipping, he wiped his mouth. "Can't remember it," he muttered, still avoiding Sophie's eyes. He could remember it. Of course he could. The words continually circled his head. Especially when he looked at Sophie. But there was no way he was going to admit it. That song wasn't meant to be heard by anyone—it was far too revealing.

"Doesn't it go something like this?" Sean cleared his throat.

> *"Never did I ever think you would be,*
> *Never did I ever see you with me,*
> *But now you have come and shown me the way*
> *Never will I ever be the same...*
> *so just stay."*

Fire burned in Josh's veins, his throat tightened and his heart thumped. "Of all of the lyrics you decide to memorise, you chose those. What is your problem? Do you hate me today or something?" he barked at his friend, shaking. "You can't even remember my number one hits, but this, *this* you bloody remember." Weren't best friends meant to stand by you in times of need? Yet here Sean was, throwing him under the bus and then making sure the bus driver reversed right back over him.

"Told you he's totally screwed up." Sean raised his eyebrows and smirked at John before taking a sip of his beer.

"Well." Josh slapped the bar top. "That's me done for the day, I think." He shook his head. "I don't think I can take any more of this…whatever *this* is." Without looking at Sophie or anyone else, he pushed away from the bar and left. He had to get away. He'd walk back to London if he had to. There was no way he was staying here. Every minute not being able to touch Sophie was bad enough, but now everyone was revelling in his torture, like they were sticking a knife in and twisting it.

As he walked down the street, his heart pounding to the beat of his footsteps, he heard his name.

Closing his eyes, he took a deep breath before turning to face his destiny. Part of him had wanted Sophie to run after him. The other part wanted the ground to swallow him whole and never spit him out again.

Sophie ran down the street, almost in slow motion, her blonde hair billowing beautifully behind her, her cheeks flushed pink.

He was fucked. He couldn't even walk away from her.

"Josh," she breathed. "Did you write that?" A deep v formed between her eyebrows. He would have given anything to massage it away with his thumb.

Thinking, he let out his breath. Lying didn't come naturally to him—he hated it. Well, lying to anyone but the media. And yet, this past week he had lied to not just the press, but to himself and even worse, to Sophie. He couldn't lie anymore.

He nodded.

Her eyes glimmered. "It's beautiful." She crossed her arms

in front of her and caressed her bottom lip with her fingers. Finally she looked up at him again. "Is it about me?"

~

Sophie gulped. Josh stood silent in front of her, staring into her soul.

Then, after an eternity, he croaked, "Yes."

All the wind in her lungs left her. Her insides felt like jelly. That must be the most romantic thing anyone had ever done for her. And yet...he had treated her like a plaything. Something to be disposed of and rejected when he no longer needed her.

"I'm confused," she admitted.

"I know." He took a step closer as if he wanted to reach out for her, his eyes wide. Then he let out a long sigh. "I have so much that I need to say to you, so much that I want to say to you. And so much to apologise for. Sean's right, I'm totally screwed. And it's all because of you."

Her heart ached, desperate for him and for the comforting words he surely wanted to offer her. But her head had to be sensible here, and protect her from any more pain. "Should we go back in then, and talk? Alone?"

"I'd love to, but only if you're okay with that."

She nodded. She couldn't just let him walk away. There was so much to talk about, so much to understand. Sure, people didn't normally sit down and discuss what had happened after a one-night stand. Especially when one of them had crept out in the middle of the night. But she needed to understand. She needed to know what had happened. Not that she had any experience with one-night stands, but this felt different.

They walked back to the pub in silence. This was about to be very awkward.

Sophie heaved the door open and walked back over to the bar, where John, Sean, Belle and James were still standing where she'd left them.

She put in their drink order. "Two Jägerbombs, John, and then whatever beer Josh was having, and a large glass of white wine for me, please." She tapped nervously on the bar top, aware of all eyes on her and Josh.

John poured the drinks and set them on the bar for Sophie, handing back the cash she'd laid down.

"Drink those slowly," he warned her, holding the notes for a brief second so she had to look up at him in understanding.

"You don't have to worry about me," she told him.

"I know I don't. He's a good guy." He nodded over to Josh.

What the hell? Weren't big brothers meant to automatically hate whatever guy their sister was with? He sure had hated Scott, and yet with Josh he was pouring him drinks and laughing with him.

Belle scoffed loudly.

"Right, that's it." James placed his half-empty glass on the bar. "I'm taking you home. You had your warning and you couldn't help yourself."

"What?" Belle retorted. "I wasn't even laughing, it was a cough." She coughed for good measure.

He grinned. "You're not fooling anyone. Come on, I'll drive you home and let your brother deal with you."

"Humph, as if he's going to do anything about it." Belle shouldered her way through them and hugged Sophie goodbye. As she wrapped her arms around her friend, she whispered, "Be sensible, don't take any crap. And text me straight after with all the details!" She turned to Josh and pointed at him. "I'm warning you, not a foot out of line!"

"That's it, Belle, come on." And James scooped up her elbow and directed her out of the pub. She leaned into him as they left, laughing at something he had said.

What was going on there? Sophie wondered. The next time she saw Belle, they needed to talk.

Josh picked up their drinks and took them over to an empty table, letting Sophie settle before sitting down himself. He handed her a Jägerbomb and they clinked their glasses together and downed them in one. The fiery liquid slipped down her throat and she shuddered, the alcohol immediately taking effect.

"I know we don't know each other, Sophie," Josh began, "but I feel like we do. Ever since I saw you, I've felt this connection to you. I hated hearing what that jerk of a boyfriend did to you. I couldn't bear thinking you would just leave the awards ceremony because of him. I wanted to protect you and see your eyes light up every time you saw something new that night. And then, when I needed it, you comforted me. Not because you were on show and wanted to impress anyone else, but because you felt that connection to me, too. Or at least that's what I thought. I was desperate for that night with you, Sophie. I texted you with jittery fingers and jumped at the first opportunity to see you again. And then the fear I felt at the irrational thought that you may have been hurt. Sophie, it tore through me. I've never known anything like it."

He sat back in his chair with a sigh, ruffling up his perfect black hair as he did so. He looked as distraught as he had that night he came banging on her hotel door. And just like that night, she had a sudden urge to reach out to him, to try and comfort him. But she needed to hear him out, so instead she gripped her glass tighter.

"And then you were fine, and I felt stupid but relieved," he said. "All the rules I have for myself flew out the window, and I couldn't help myself. It was amazing. *You* were amazing. But I do have rules, Sophie. I broke them, but they're there for a reason. To protect me, to protect you. And that's why I left. So

I didn't break any more of them, to protect you from me, from this poisonous world that I live in."

Sophie let him speak, memorising every word as her hands shook on the stem of her wine glass. He wanted her, but he wasn't allowing himself to have her. "Josh, you didn't protect me. When I needed you to protect me from the media, you didn't, you made it worse. You walked away from me without a second thought."

"I did think about you. I do think about you. But you not being with me is better for you."

"Who are you to decide my life for me?" She clenched her jaw and shook her head. "You assumed I wanted more from you, that I would want another night or to have a relationship. But I didn't. It was one night, Josh. One night I wish didn't happen."

That wasn't strictly true. She looked down at the table, hiding her face from him. She hadn't meant to sleep with him and she didn't know what she wanted from him. But she wasn't a one-night stand sort of woman. Although she didn't regret spending the night with him—after all, it was the most amazing night she'd ever had—she did regret everything that had followed.

"Don't say that." He was quiet, his usually bright green eyes now dull.

"I don't think you get how much this has affected me. I could have lost my job. I've probably lost my opportunity to finally get the promotion that I've been working towards for years. And I have sure as hell lost everyone's respect." Tears welled in her eyes, but she ignored them, letting them pool and drop slowly down her flushed cheeks.

"I wanted to protect you," he replied, defensively.

"But you didn't!" She slapped the table. Why couldn't he see that his protection had hurt her more? "You made it worse, Josh."

"I'm sorry, Sophie." He reached across the table and held onto her fingers ever so softly, as if he was scared to break her any further.

"You keep saying that, but it doesn't make it better." She wrenched her fingers from him. Whenever they touched, her body zinged, and she couldn't bear to feel that right now.

"I know."

"And now you've shown up and turned my world upside down again. What am I meant to think? Did you know I would be here? Are you trying to torture me more? And then you wrote a song about me? You say you don't want to hurt me, but you are and you keep hurting me!" Tears spilled freely down her cheeks and she put her palms over her eyes to stop them and leant her elbows on the table, desperate to not see him, to not see everyone staring at her crying, desperate for the pain to stop.

The cushion next to her on the bench seat dipped and she felt a thigh squash against hers, an arm wrap around her back and a cheek rest against her head. Despite herself, she leant into Josh and took the comfort he offered her. He kissed her head and stroked her hair, letting her sit in silence and breathe through her emotions.

Something about him sitting next to her, just being with her, was so natural, so comforting. Even though her head told her that she should distance herself from him, her heart wanted to keep him close.

"I don't know what to think," she croaked.

"I know, Soph. All I know is that I just want to be here, right now, with you."

"Me too," she whispered, snuggling into him. He had caused all of this pain. Surely he could take it all away?

"Well then, we'll just be."

He settled back on the bench with her in the nook of his neck, tracing small circles on her hip. After a short while of silence, Sophie's tears finally dried and her heart returned to beating normally. Then Josh whispered, "Your brother is staring at us."

"He just wants me to be okay." She didn't even bother looking up. "He's always been there to protect me, but he soon realised when I was an adult he couldn't look out for me in the same way anymore. He hated Scott. But he's gone easy on you."

"Has he?"

"Believe it or not, yes he has."

"Sophie?" Josh asked, tilting her chin up to look at him. "I would really like to see you again. I know you probably don't want to and I completely understand that and won't pressure you, but I can't just leave you again." He stared into her eyes, searching for something in them as his thumb traced her lower lip.

"Okay," she whispered.

There was something about this man sitting next to her. He was irresistible. And it wasn't even that he was Josh Heart, singer-songwriter extraordinaire. That part didn't appeal to her at all. It was just Josh that she wanted to be around. Just Josh that she wanted to get to know. She was drawn to him like a magnet.

Boy, she was in trouble. She couldn't even walk away from him after one night. Not even after everything he had done to her.

"Really?" A smile broke through his frown.

"Really. I thought you had rules, though."

"You make me want to break all of them." Lowering his head, he bent forwards and kissed her, ever so slightly and ever so quickly.

CHAPTER 12

Josh stared at himself in his rearview mirror. *You've got this. Why are you so nervous?* He wiped his palms down his black jeans again. *You want her, and she wants you. This is easy. You're just an average guy on a date. A date with a woman you have already hurt and happen to be crazy about. Fuck!* He thumped his fist on his steering wheel. He was going to screw this up…again.

Blowing out a frustrated breath, he opened his car door in the darkening hours of the evening. The peacefulness of the street engulfed him. He'd lived in London since signing with his record label. What would life be like in a little village like this? He scanned the street for the familiar glint of a camera lens. Nothing.

He took long, impatient strides to Sophie's door, where he knocked and scanned the street again for good measure. Force of habit.

Sophie's beaming smile and bright blue eyes welcomed him as she opened the door. Dark skinny jeans clung to her legs like a second skin and she wore a cream, off-the-shoulder jumper. Every time he saw her, she mesmerised him, settling herself firmly in his heart, clinging to his being. He would break every rule in his book for this woman.

Her eyes widened ever so slightly as he devoured her in one look, not saying a word. Shaking himself from his wild thoughts, he bent towards her and kissed her lightly on the cheek. Fruity, floral notes tickled his nose, an intoxicating smell he wanted to lap up from her skin.

God. There was no way he was going to survive the night without touching her in the ways he wanted.

"You look beautiful as ever," he whispered in her ear. "Are you ready to leave?"

She took her raincoat from a coat hook, and then he had to stifle the groan that almost escaped him at the sight of her arse as she bent down to grab her bag.

"You alright?" she asked him, raising an eyebrow.

Fuck, had he just groaned out loud?

"Course," he replied, stuffing his hands into his pockets.

"You haven't told me where we're going yet," she said as she locked the door behind them.

He offered her his arm as they walked to his car down the street. He hadn't wanted to park it directly out the front of her house in case paparazzi had followed him here. "That's because it's a surprise." Sophie wrinkled her nose, and he chuckled at her. "What? Do you not like surprises?"

"No one's ever surprised me before." She shrugged.

He shook his head. Why had no one ever treated her like the princess she deserved to be treated as? He twirled her around, knowing it worked wonders to break her mind from spiralling into bad thoughts. She giggled with glee.

"Your carriage awaits, my lady." He opened the door for her, certain she had never had that common courtesy either.

"Woah!" She stopped dead in her tracks, her smile falling, her eyes widening. "Is that your car?"

He stared at the open door in his grip. He hadn't thought twice about his car tonight, but maybe he should have.

"Is that an Aston Martin?" She skirted around the car, as if afraid to get too close.

"Well, I hope it's my car, otherwise we're about to commit a crime." He straightened up.

"It's beautiful," she whispered, through her fingers that caressed her lips. "I've always wanted to go in an Aston Martin."

For a moment, Josh froze. Did she think he was too flashy, or worse, did she want him to be just that? Shutting down the inner voice whispering in his ear—the one telling him to protect himself and her by speeding off into the sunset—he reached for her hand. Her fingers curled around his and he held on, centring himself again. He met her eyes, the cool blue twinkling back at him under the streetlight.

This was Sophie. His Sophie. She didn't want him for his fame, his glory, his money.

Do not let your past ruin your future.

Pulling her to him, he kissed her on the lips, needing to feel her realness. Her soft lips opened for him with a groan as his tongue explored her. His hands caressed her hips and cupped her arse.

She was pure heaven.

Then he pulled away from her, and held her hand as he ushered her into the passenger seat and closed the door. How was he going to control himself?

Sophie had never been in such a luxurious car. As Josh drove through the night, following the satnav directions along the dark, winding country lanes, the leather seats hugged her body and she sat so low to the floor she could feel the vibrations of the engine from her toes to her head. She clung to the handle and the seat, feeling the power around her, all at Josh's control. He drove steadily, but if he wanted to floor it, she knew she'd be pushed back into her seat.

All her life she had aspired to own an Aston Martin. But shortly after deciding her career lay in teaching, she realised she would never be able to afford one. And now, she couldn't be happier with her little Fiat. She was too much of a scaredy cat for all this power.

They sat in silence, listening to the radio as Josh followed the directions, humming along and tapping on his steering wheel. He seemed to be brooding on something, but she couldn't tell what. The silence was welcome though—she needed a minute to compose herself after that kiss. God, he knew just how to turn her insides to lava. Her whole body thrummed. Even now, it called to him to kiss her again.

"We're getting close." He laid his hand over the one she had on her seat.

"Well, I'm glad you're driving. I've lived here all my life and I have no clue where we are." The sky was now pitch black outside and the full moon lit their way with a smattering of stars glistening above them.

Josh pulled off the road through a small opening, the car bumping along a track, the keys clattering against the steering column. "Hold on tight," he told her. "I don't want you banging your head." He gripped the steering wheel, his eyes narrowing in on the dark track surrounded by trees and bushes either side. "I hope we don't bottom out," he muttered.

Eventually, after a couple of bumpy minutes where Josh swore a handful of times, the headlights lit up a beautiful barn in a small clearing. Spotlights lit the barn from the ground, casting a welcoming glow on the historic building. It must have been a few hundred years old.

As she sat in awe, staring at the thatched roof and rough

wooden cladding, Josh skirted around the car and opened the door for her. He held her hand as she stepped out onto the gravel pathway.

Then he guided her to the entranceway and opened the large, heavy, wooden door for her to walk through.

If there was any breath left in her lungs, it immediately left her as she walked into the old barn. The exposed rafters loomed above her, the eaves intertwined. The large space was empty, apart from a small table set for two in the middle of the barn. Large panes of glass were set into the wall on the other side of the table, showing the most wonderful view of the dark countryside and hills below them. In front of the windows sat bales of hay and blankets, and all around them, twinkly lights and candles adorned every wooden pillar possible.

"This place is incredible," Sophie breathed.

"It's all for you." Josh snuggled into her hair.

She searched around. "No one else is here?"

Josh shook his head slowly, a small smile tugging at his lips. "Just us. Come." He took her by the hand, gently directing her to take a seat at the table. A large wicker picnic basket sat next to it, and Josh opened it to reveal a bottle of red wine and some plates of food.

"What is all of this?" Sophie asked, searching the basket of goodies.

"Dinner." He poured them out a glass of wine each.

"Is it potatoes and onions in five ways?" She smiled at him.

He laughed, a sound that shot joy straight to her heart. "No, nothing so extravagant. Just a picnic dinner." He pulled out quiche and potatoes, pickles, cheese and meats. The food seemed never-ending. "And, of course..." He brought out a plate with a silver cloche on top, holding it out for Sophie to uncover it. "Dessert."

She lifted the cloche and found a chocolate torte, with

chocolate pastry and a cocoa powder covering, sitting on the plate. She salivated.

"All for you." Josh took the cloche from her and covered the dessert back up. "After dinner, of course." He winked.

He started piling food on a plate for her, much higher than she would have ever dished out for herself. She sipped her wine, calming the nerves that bubbled inside her. "If I'm to eat a whole dessert by myself, I won't be able to eat that much dinner!"

He added another spoonful of buttery new potatoes. "I'm sure you'll manage." Finally finished, he raised his wine glass to chime against hers. "To us."

The sound of their glasses tinkled across the softly lit barn. "To us," she replied, hypnotised by his eyes, the amber flecks growing before her. "How did you manage to pull this all off in twenty-four hours?" she asked, slicing into her dinner.

"That's the great thing about my job. I get to do what I like. So today, I planned this." He shrugged as if it were no hardship at all.

She smiled at how different their worlds were. Her day had consisted of settling an argument between Rebecca and Autumn over who was the best at cartwheeling, and celebrating with Harry when he finally achieved ten out of ten on his spelling. For all the money in the world, she wouldn't swap her work for anything. It was what she lived for.

"How did you sort this place out at the last minute?" she asked.

"I just searched the internet and made some phone calls." He shrugged again. "It's a wedding venue, apparently."

She looked around the pretty space again. "It's a beautiful place for a wedding." She sighed, seeing exactly where the top table would go and imagining the dance floor in front of the large windows.

"Do you want to get married?" Josh asked.

Sophie snapped her head round to him, her eyes wide and her eyebrows halfway up to her hairline. Josh loaded potatoes and meat onto his fork, not looking at her, and she settled slightly. Good, he hadn't just proposed to her.

"I suppose one day," she replied, once her heart rate settled back again. "What about you?"

"I hadn't really thought about it before, to be honest."

Sophie had seen all the women he'd been pictured with in the glossy gossip mags. The pain in her heart felt as if she had just picked up her knife and stabbed it between her ribs. She took a large gulp of her wine.

Then he looked into her eyes. "I suppose when you find the right person, it's something you start to think about."

She broke away from his gaze and placed a piece of cheese into her mouth, not tasting a single bit of it. When she had first gone out with Scott, she'd wondered if he was the one and if they would ever get married. Part of her had hoped that was their future. But as their relationship went on, that little glimmer faded until she had known they would never get married.

And when she met Josh? Well…he had been wearing a suit, so there was no denying how good he would look on his wedding day. But more than that? Could she see herself standing next to him at the altar, swapping vows and placing a ring on his finger?

She blinked into the darkness of the window, following the small headlights of a car on a road down in the valley.

Light fingers stroked the back of her hand. She twisted her head back to Josh, who was gazing at her, a glint in his eye.

"Daydreaming?" he asked her softly.

She shook her head, ridding herself of visions she didn't want to think about or admit to. "Sorry."

"How was your day?" He tactfully changed the topic.

"Better than last Monday, for sure." Josh's skin blanched.

"I'm not saying that to bring up everything," she backtracked. "It's just that last Monday was horrible, what with everyone throwing shady looks at me and the 'talk' my boss had with me."

"I understand. I'm sorry." Josh laid his knife and fork on his plate.

"You don't have to apologise again. I meant it when I said we would start afresh."

They had promised each other to act as if nothing had happened between them and this was their first date, which in reality it was.

She gripped his hand, offering him comfort. "Is it time for dessert now?" she asked, bringing a light-hearted tone back into the room.

He grinned at her. "You're amazing, do you know that?" She felt her cheeks redden. Bending down, he rescued the chocolate torte from the bottom of the picnic basket and swapped it with her plate. "Enjoy." He handed her a fork.

"Are you seriously not going to eat any of this?" How could anyone turn down chocolate?

He shook his head. "It's all for you. And anything you don't eat you can take home with you and have over the next couple of days."

"I'm still not sure if I can be friends with anyone who doesn't like chocolate." She smirked as she scooped her fork through the chocolatey goodness and the crumbly crust. Her mouth salivated again. Taking a large piece, she eyed the dessert as she slowly placed it in her mouth, savouring every last morsel. The chocolate melted away on her tongue, and she was in heaven. Moaning, she closed her eyes, willing it to last forever.

But as with all good things, it had to come to an end. She opened her eyes to reload her fork but was stopped by Josh staring at her through his lashes, his mouth slightly parted.

"Do you want some?" she asked, knowing he was missing out on a tiny slice of heaven. He shook his head, the green in his eyes darkening. "Come on, you have to try a little bit. Just for me?" She scooped a tiny bit of torte onto the fork and offered it to him to eat. His eyes never left hers as he opened his mouth and took the morsel.

He chewed slowly, seeming to savour the sight of her as much as he savoured the food. "You really are the most amazing woman I have ever met," he told her, leaning forward to kiss her. Their tongues swirled around each other. His kiss was so soft, so sweet, her insides tingled, wanting him to touch her with his hands in the same way his tongue did. When they broke apart, his hand cupped her cheek. "You have converted me. I do like chocolate," he whispered softly, rubbing his nose against hers. "When it's on your tongue." And he kissed her again.

Josh hadn't thought he could stop kissing Sophie. It had taken all of his willpower to do so. The taste of chocolate mixed in with the pure taste of Sophie was unlike anything he'd ever experienced before. He would feed her chocolate every day if it made her happy and he could devour her mouth afterwards.

Finally his brain had kicked in. She loved chocolate dessert so much, it was mean of him to not let her finish.

He sat back in his chair, watching her eating her fair share of the torte, unable to look away.

Eventually she laid her fork down and declared she had finished. Silently taking her hand, Josh guided her over to the hay bales and blankets and settled her against him, leaning against his chest. They sat on the floor and watched the darkness outside, both absorbed in a world they could hardly see. Lazily tapping a tune on Sophie's hip, Josh had never been so content.

"So, I met your brother John. Do I have any other brothers to worry about?"

Sophie turned her head up to gaze at him, just about in kissing distance. "No, it's just me and John."

"You two seem really close."

"We are. He's always looked out for me, supported me, been there whenever I needed him. He's the best big brother."

Josh saw through the small smile on her face that didn't quite reach her eyes. "What about your parents? Are you close to them?" Her eyes dulled even more. There was no doubt he had found the source of that pain.

"My mum died about ten years ago now, just when I had finished university." She turned her head again to look out the window. "And my dad left us when I was two years old. We haven't heard from him since."

"I'm sorry, Sophie." Josh kissed her hair, smoothing it away on her shoulders.

"Don't be, it's no one's fault. John was my father figure, the one I ran to when I had car trouble, the one who taught me how to ride my bike, the one who cuddled me when I had nightmares."

"What about your mum?"

"She was caring and loving in her own way, but she had to work hard to cover all the bills and keep us in our home. And when she wasn't working, she spent her time going out with different men. None of them stayed put. She was always moving on, trying to find something she didn't have at home."

Josh's heart tore for Sophie, and for John. What a childhood to have. Far different from the one he'd had, where his biggest worry had been if he'd get a new guitar for Christmas. "I'm glad you had John." He pulled her in closer.

"Me too, but John doesn't have anyone, and that always upsets me."

"Does he have a partner now?"

"No, he doesn't really date anyone. I'm sure he has his flings and is quite the ladies' man, but nothing sticks."

"His time will come." Josh was certain of it.

"I hope so," Sophie mumbled. "Anyway, what about your family?"

"I have my little sister Lizzie, who isn't so little anymore. She must be twenty-five now, so there's a big age gap between us. And my mum and dad are still together. I moved away when I got my record deal and I probably don't visit them as much as I should." He hadn't ever thought about it before, and he certainly hadn't felt the nagging guilt that now settled itself in his stomach. He had pushed aside his old life in favour of this one. But what did he have to show for it, apart from a handful of fast cars, a swanky London house and a few golden trophies in his cabinet? "What about your future?"

"I don't know anymore," Sophie sighed. "I thought I knew what I wanted and how my life would be, but this past week has shown I can't rely on that picture. Who knows what my future will look like."

After a short while of brooding silence, Josh moved, his bum growing numb on the floor. "I should get you back. It's a school night after all."

"Yes." Sophie stifled a yawn. "It's been wonderful, thank you so much. I couldn't have wished for anything more perfect."

"Do you like surprises now?" He grabbed the last of the dessert and led her back through the front door, out into the cold night air.

"Most definitely. Do we not have to tidy up?" She looked back as he opened the car door for her once again.

"No, that will all be taken care of."

The night had been wonderful. Sophie couldn't think of a single thing Josh could have done to make it any better. Despite all that, she struggled to keep her eyes open on the way home, with the warm car heaters blowing in her face and the leather seats wrapping around her like a hug. Josh let her sit in silence, driving her back to reality.

She didn't know what this was between them, what it would turn out to be. She had probably just delayed her heartache by a few extra weeks. After all, he was Josh Heart. And she was just Sophie.

But something told her she needed this time with him. Needed these experiences with him. Even if he did leave her and the pain was a hundred times worse than it had been before. Eventually, she drifted off to sleep.

She was woken by a gentle shake on her arm and whispers of her name. "Sophie. Sophie. We're home."

Home. She rubbed her eyes, brushing the sleepiness away. "What a bad date I am, falling asleep on you. You must think I'm so boring."

Josh's cheeky grin lit the car up. "Don't be silly, you're

anything but boring. Come on." He undid her seat belt for her. "Let me walk you to the door."

Jumping out of the car, he practically sprinted around it to let her out the other side. He offered her his arm and they walked along the dark street to her door, where Sophie rustled in her bag for her front door keys.

She didn't want him to leave just yet. But she had no idea how to get him to stay. There was a tension between them and it hardened as they reached her door. It seemed like they were both aware they were on the edge of something. Neither of them spoke.

Sophie placed her key into the lock and twisted, the clattering keys echoing off the silent houses all around them. Without opening the door, she turned to Josh—his eyes drinking in her every move—and blurted out what she wanted to say. "Did you want to come in?"

He nodded, his eyes darker than the night sky above them.

She let him through and closed the door. "Did you want a hot drink?" she asked as she hung her bag on a hook in the hallway. He hung his jacket up next to hers.

"A coffee would be great, to wake me up for the drive home."

Her heart took a nosedive. She didn't want him to leave. Walking through to her kitchen, she busied her hands making him a hot drink, settling for a cold glass of water for herself to wash away the slightly hazy feeling that came with drinking that large glass of red wine and sleeping in the car. Maybe just a small part of it had come from being around Josh too.

He had followed her into the kitchen and was inspecting the photographs she had stuck on her fridge with brightly coloured magnets. "Is this you and John as kids?" He pointed to the one of them at Christmas. John was helping her with her new make-up set by being her dummy, the bright-blue eyeshadow and pink-smudged lipstick all over his face. Sophie smiled, nodding. He really was the best big brother.

"And this is you and your friend?"

"Belle, yes." They sat side by side in the park, school uniforms on, skirts rolled up short, ties skewed to the side, hugging each other. "We've been friends since school."

"She doesn't look so angry here." Josh smiled and leant back against the counter, watching her pour the boiling water into a mug.

"She's always been hot-headed." Sophie stirred the coffee. "And she is very protective."

"I can tell that." He took the mug from her, brushing her fingers with his as he took it.

"But you don't have to worry about seeing her again."

The brush of his skin against hers sent her insides warming up, the pool of desire getting deeper. She really didn't want him to leave. And she'd thought inviting him in for coffee would make that clear. But it seemed like he just wanted his caffeine fix and he would be on his way.

She chewed on her lip, focusing on the corner of one of the photos where the paper was starting to peel up in old age.

"Hey? What's going on?" Josh's soft voice brought her from her thoughts.

She had no idea why she said it, but she blurted out, "Do you not want to stay?" She immediately cringed inside—he probably had a date tomorrow night with a model or something.

"I'm staying for coffee, aren't I?" His eyes twinkled as he sipped his drink.

What was happening to her? She wanted so much more than for him to stay for one coffee. "I thought you might want to stay for longer," she said quietly, her cheeks heating up. She turned from him, mortified that he would be able to see her desire burning bright in her eyes.

"It's not that I don't want to," he began.

But before her heart could plummet any more, and he rejected her, she shrugged and said, "It's fine. I get it. You really don't have to explain." But she could tell her voice was a little bit too loud and a little bit too croaky to fool anyone into thinking she was fine.

"Hey." Josh pulled her to him. "It's because I don't want to force you to spend the night with me, because I promised myself I would treat you right, like a lady, and because you're working tomorrow and I didn't want to keep you up." He brushed a strand of hair from her face. "Sophie, I want you, and I want to see where this goes."

She stared into his eyes, focusing on the amber flecks sprinkled amongst the green. "What's going to happen between us?" she breathed, desperately hoping that he had all the answers.

"I don't know, Soph." He brushed her bottom lip. "I can't promise anything for our future—neither of us can know what's going to happen. But I can promise you all of me, right now, and tomorrow and the next day and the day after that. Until you decide you don't want me anymore."

"What if you decide you don't want me anymore?"

His luscious lips curled up on one side. "I can't see that happening, Sophie. I can't stop thinking about you, haven't been able to since I first laid eyes on you in those bright studio lights, the camera snapping away." He pulled her body to his, hugging her closer. "And as for meeting Belle again, as much as it scares me, I want to change her mind. I want to show her I can treat you the way you deserve. I want to show that to John too, to show everyone you love and care about that I'm right for you."

"Well then," she said, her heart fluttering full of feelings she couldn't possibly describe. "You'll probably need to meet Tony, too."

Josh pulled back abruptly. "Who's Tony?"

"He owns the pub we were in yesterday, but he's like a surrogate big brother to me. He's just as protective of me as John and Belle are."

Josh groaned, slumping against the counter. "Oh God, as grateful as I am that you have so much support and love around you, you sure are making my life more difficult!" He chuckled, his toned abs pulsing under her hand. "So, three people? Three people who already hate me, who I have to impress and change their minds?"

"Yep, but I'm sure that will be easy for a celebrity like you!"

He tickled her under the ribs, making her shriek in delight. And then he kissed her, lightly at first, but when his fingers stopped moving, his lips hardened against hers, their tongues swirling together.

"I should get going," he whispered, resting his nose against hers, closing his eyes.

"You're not staying?" She rubbed her nose softly against his.

"I promised myself that I wouldn't stay, that we need to take this slowly."

That knot of desire deep inside her belly must be making her crazy. She couldn't think straight. And she certainly couldn't be expected to feel properly. Right now him leaving felt like a rejection she wasn't sure she could bear.

"Why do you always think you know what's best for me? The more you try to protect me the more you hurt me." She pushed away from him and picked up his half-drunk coffee and chucked it down the sink.

"Soph, I didn't think you'd want me here. I thought you wanted to take things slowly and see how it goes."

"You haven't asked, you just assume. One minute you talk about meeting my friends and spending every day with me, and kiss me like that. And then the next minute you push me away."

"Soph, I just want to protect you." He tried to grasp her arm.

"How did that work out last time, Josh?" She pulled away from his hand, her jaw clenched tight.

Josh sighed, letting his hand fall, hitting his thigh. "You're right. It didn't work last time, and it doesn't look like it will work this time."

"So just take what you want. Be honest." She stepped towards him, challenging him.

"You don't want to tempt me, Sophie." His voice all but smouldered, husky and quiet. The green of his eyes burned bright.

"Oh, but I do." She wasn't used to taking charge in the bedroom, but now she pushed her body against his, determined to make something happen.

He stifled a groan. "Please don't tempt me." The husky edge in his voice turned to a plea, his eyebrows drawn together as if he were in actual pain. "I didn't bring a condom."

She smirked up at him. "It's your lucky night. I have some."

"Some from before, or some that you bought today?"

She wasn't sure why it mattered. "Today."

And with that simple word, Josh pounced on her.

CHAPTER 14

Scooping Sophie's legs from underneath her, Josh carried her out of the kitchen to the stairs. She clung to his neck, giggling uncontrollably.

The sheer relief at hearing she had bought condoms today —for them—sent his mind reeling. That meant she had wanted him, hoped for him. They weren't just backups for her ex-boyfriend, or for anyone else. They were bought for him… for this. The little admission sent all the blood in his body to one place. And that one place demanded he now act. *Finally.*

He carried her up the stairs with ease, not even breaking a sweat. As he searched the landing and all the closed doors, Sophie pointed to the furthest one. "That one."

He crossed the floor in three strides. Pushing open the door, he carried her over the threshold, an image clearly in his mind of holding her, just like this in some near future, with her all dressed in white. How had this woman infected his mind?

He threw her onto the bed, and she shrieked in glee. His heart expanded as he witnessed the sheer joy pouring from her.

She started unbuttoning his jeans and pulling at his shirt, but he held her wrists still, gazing at the pure desire oozing from every pore of her body. Dropping her wrists, he held her still with his gaze, then he knelt in front of her and lifted her top, exposing her pale blue, lacy bra. That first night they had together, he had devoured her so quickly he never had the chance to memorise her, to savour her.

Now he had that chance, and he wasn't going to miss a moment.

Reaching around her back, he unhooked her bra and pulled the straps from her shoulders, exposing her breasts. Fuck, she was incredible. Her nipples hardened before him, the soft skin rising in bumps as he rubbed the buds with his thumbs ever so lightly. She moaned at his touch. Incredible.

Pushing her back gently, he undid her jeans and pulled them from her to find matching lacy blue knickers beneath.

He touched her softly, tracing the slight curve of her hips, her tummy, committing to memory the way her ribs expanded when she breathed, the little mole on the underside of her left breast. This woman was a goddess, and she was his. He had to keep her.

He peeled her panties away to reveal her fully to him. She lay there, silent, watching his every move as if she were memorising him too.

He crawled up her body, careful not to touch her. "You're amazing, Sophie." Words normally came so easy to him, but now, with her, he knew he would never be able to express what he felt for her.

She fluttered her eyelashes closed and tilted her chin up. As soon as they kissed, there would be no stopping him. He leant down and took her lips with his, his hands returning to caress her. Every touch growing bolder than the one before. Every touch exploring more of her skin.

She wrapped her arms around his neck, pressing her naked

body against his clothed one. Her hands fumbled with the buttons on his shirt, undoing them one by one, and then pushing the shirt from him. Josh stood, and her hands came to his trousers and boxers, helping him lower them to the floor. He bent down to take his socks off and then jumped back onto the bed and moulded his body against hers.

He smoothed his hands over her warm body, goosebumps erupting from where his hands trailed. He flicked her hard nipples under his thumbs, making her writhe with need beside him.

Kissing her, playing with her, was unlike anything he had ever experienced before. Twisting so he lay on top of her, he then pushed her legs apart. She held his eyes, not saying a word. He reached down to her opening, wet and slick, ready for him.

As soon as he touched her tender flesh, her eyes widened, her breath hitching. Her body stilled for the slightest second as his fingers entered her, before her carnal desires took over her body and she moaned and moved beneath him. As he caressed her slowly and gently, her body bucked harder, egging him on. But he wouldn't give in to her. Not yet.

Wrapping her arms around his shoulders, she tugged at him to act quicker. The more she pulled, the slower he went. The more she bucked, the softer his touch.

"Josh," she groaned, pleading for more.

"I told you not to tempt me." He nuzzled and sucked her ear lobe.

"Please, Josh," she moaned again, wriggling her hips to try and get some satisfaction.

"I know, baby." He kissed her neck, his fingers fluttering inside her. "I will make you come. I promise. But first…" He kissed the other side of her neck. "I'm going to make you weak with need, I'm going to make you beg for release, and only when you think you can't take any more, then I'll make you come."

"I'll do it myself then." The defiance lit in Sophie's eyes as she sent her hands down to her opening. But Josh caught her tiny wrists in one hand and wrenched them above her head. His other hand stayed between her legs, now deadly still.

"Nice try, but now you'll pay for that." He licked his way down to her nipples, still holding her wrists. She shivered as he swirled her bud in his mouth. He mirrored the movement of his tongue with his fingers, using his thumb to caress her clitoris. She started to pant, her head swishing from side to side, her eyes rolling back. He sped up his fingers and his tongue, and Sophie's moans escaped her.

Releasing her nipple, he kissed her harshly, his tongue swirling hers like he had her nipple. He nipped and bit at her lips as his fingers traced her insides, keeping hold of that spot she loved so much, pushing and pulsing harder and faster. She bucked uncontrollably beneath him.

"Come now, Sophie," he demanded. And she split, screaming his name into the quiet room. Her insides pulsed around him, her now free fingers digging into his shoulders to keep him in place. Gradually her grip eased, her insides relaxed and her limbs went limp.

"Wow," she breathed, her breasts heaving, her arm resting over her eyes.

"Where are the condoms?" he whispered. She pointed at the bedside table. Pulling open the drawer, he saw a whole new box waiting for him. God, she was perfect. Grabbing one, he ripped it open and pulled it onto himself.

Sophie heard the ripping of the foil packet, felt the bed move beside her as Josh came back to join her. Her body still tingled from her orgasm, her insides still thumped. Never had she felt something so exquisite as that. He was a magician, he had to be.

He planted small kisses on her lips, trying to wake her from her drowsy state. She wasn't sure she could move a muscle, let alone open her eyes.

"I'm not sure I have the strength," she admitted, her words falling lazily from her.

Josh nudged her nose with his. "I know you do, Sophie. I want to feel you wrapped around me, to inch into you, to make you throb and smoulder." The pulse in her neck quickened despite herself, her body warming all over. Josh found her racing pulse point and licked. "I want you to scream my name again. I want to hold you close while we come together. I want you to forget everything, everyone, but me and right now."

She wrapped her arms around his neck. How could he be making her so turned on with just words? A thumb flicked across her nipple.

"Your body wants me, Sophie. I can see it. You're breathing heavier, your pulse is racing, your nipples are hard, and I bet, if I was to feel between your legs, you would still be wet for me." She shook her head. "You don't think so? Let's see, shall we?" He took her hand in his and guided her fingers with him, down to her folds. Guiding them, he made her feel herself from top to bottom, her juices coating both their fingers. "What do you think, Sophie?" He nibbled on her ear lobe. "Are you tempting me again?" She moaned despite herself, and he spread her legs with his thighs, positioning himself at her entrance.

"Josh?" She opened her eyes at last, drinking in the sight of him.

"Yes." His eyes devoured her.

"Take me."

As he pushed himself slowly into her, his grin lit the room, and lit a place in her heart she didn't know was there. Slower than anything she had known before, he moved, building her up at an agonising pace.

"Josh," she pleaded, "please."

Kissing her, he sped up just a bit to match her thrusting hips. He nuzzled her neck, planting kisses and licks all over her. Their hands found each other and intertwined. This wasn't hot, steamy, raunchy, one-night stand sex. This was making love, this was coming together as one, cherishing every moment together, memorising the feel of each other. How could she protect her heart against this?

He had found her sweet spot, and all too soon she could feel the waves of ecstasy floating across her body, her insides clenching around him. Her fingers dug into his shoulders and back, spurring him on.

Up and up and up they went, Sophie shattering around him and Josh following her straight after.

Slumping down onto her, Josh collapsed. She lay limp from exhaustion. Her muscles were going to pay for that tomorrow. He rolled off her, her body instantly missing his.

After a minute of silence, she was aware of Josh moving around her, and then she was lifted like a feather, placed on her pillow and wrapped in the duvet. The bed dipped next to her, and that perfect, hard body spooned her back, bringing her in close and wrapping his warmth around her.

Neither of them spoke. They didn't need to say any words.

CHAPTER 15

The loud beeping of the wretched alarm awoke Sophie from the best sleep of her life. Reaching her arm out into the cold morning air, she hit the snooze button. Twisting around, she reached out for Josh, feeling for him in the clouds of her duvet. Her hand found nothing. Opening her eyes in the bright morning sunshine that streamed through a crack in her curtains, she couldn't see any sign of him.

Her heart plummeted. He couldn't have left her again. Not after last night. They'd connected. Hadn't they?

Sitting up in bed, she searched for any of his belongings. Not even a sock. How could he? Why had she been so stupid?

Throwing the cover off, she grabbed her dressing gown from her chair and wrapped it around herself, pulling the cord tight as if to stop the flow of tears that wanted to surface. She would not cry over him, not again.

A scalding-hot shower was what she needed. She went to the door and spotted a little white piece of paper on the other bedside table. Reaching out for it with a shaking hand, she saw a scrawly, handwritten 'Sophie' staring back at her.

She sat on the bed and opened the note.

· · ·

Sophie,

I know you probably panicked when you woke and realised I had left...again. But I had to leave as I have a meeting first thing this morning. I tried to wake you before I left but you didn't even move a muscle.

Already I don't want to leave you.

When can I see you again?

Josh

Sophie held the note to her heart, its racing starting to slow. He hadn't left her again. They had connected last night.

Unable to resist a moment longer, she grabbed her phone and called him with a big smile.

After a couple of rings, Josh answered. "Morning, beautiful."

How could he make her swoon when they weren't even together? "M-morning," she stuttered, unable to remember what she wanted to say.

"You found my note then?"

She could hear his drumming on the steering wheel.

"Yes."

"And you're not mad?"

"Well, I was before I found the note. But now, no. But I'm sad I didn't get to say goodbye." She shuffled her feet on the bare wood floor.

"I didn't want to wake you, and then I couldn't resist. But you wouldn't wake up."

"You should have tried harder." She chewed on her lip. She would give anything to have him right back with her.

"When can I see you again?"

"Well, when are you free?"

"Tonight?"

Her heart skipped a beat. "I'm free tonight." Let's be honest, even if she did have plans she would have cancelled them.

"Can I come and cook dinner for you?" he asked.

"As if you would even have to ask. I should be home by four, so come when you like."

"I'll be there at four." He paused. "Have a lovely day, Sophie."

"You too." She ended their call and squealed in delight, stomping her feet on the floor with excitement. This couldn't be real life, could it?

~

Sophie was sure she glided on air the whole day, waltzing around the classroom and never once losing her temper, not even when Billy ripped his exercise book up and chucked it all on the floor.

At three thirty, with her classroom tidy and prepared for the following day, she grabbed her bag. Ducking her head, she legged it out the door.

"Sophie?"

She stopped cold. *Bugger.* She turned around to face the headmistress, Claire Waters, a stern-looking lady with greying hair and glasses perched on the end of her nose.

"Hello." Sophie twisted the strap of her handbag.

"I was just wondering if we could have a catch up after last week?"

Dread settled in the bottom of her stomach. As much as she wanted to dart out of there to see Josh, she couldn't really say no to her boss.

"I have a doctor's appointment at four," she lied. "But I can stay for a few minutes."

Claire nodded, then turned her back and led Sophie to her

office, not saying a word. Sophie followed her like a student in trouble.

"So," Claire finally said once the door had closed behind them. "We haven't had any more disastrous headlines appear over the weekend. Which I'm very glad about." Once seated at her desk, Claire steepled her fingers in front of her chin and stared at Sophie.

"Like I said last week, unfortunately I was in the wrong place at the wrong time and got caught up in it all."

"Well, yes, I'm pleased to know you aren't seeing him. The whole raucousness caused among the parents, teachers and governors was very disruptive, don't you think?"

Sophie's body seared. She wasn't used to lying—she'd never really had to. Not since she was sixteen and she and Belle would sneak off to watch Belle's big brother, Adam, play football. They would sit on the edge of the woods, watching and drinking stolen spirits from her mum's cabinet.

"Uh-huh," she murmured in agreement, hoping silence would be the best option here. "Well, I really do think I should make a quick move for my doctor's appointment, in case there's traffic."

She rose from the chair. How long would she be questioned about all this when it was no one's business? What would happen if she and Josh did stay together and her face turned up in the paper again? Her stomach turned over. Why did he have to be a celebrity?

"Of course. We can catch up again next week?" Claire rose from her desk too.

Great, so now she was being watched like a hawk.

Sophie smiled and walked away, all her happiness having left her body. Why wasn't life ever just perfect?

She drove home, obsessing about what the future would pan out to be. Which was ridiculous—she had spent years with Scott and never obsessed so much. But with Josh, it felt different. Her relationship with Scott had never affected her job. Her relationship with Scott had never made the papers.

Driving down her street, she scanned the cars for Josh's Aston Martin, suddenly conscious of what the neighbours would think. Nothing. It was four o'clock. Maybe he'd hit traffic. She pulled into her drive and rested her head against the headrest for a couple of minutes, her eyes closed, thinking.

Just calm down and breathe. You don't need to know what the future holds, you only need to think about today. Whatever this is with Josh, there doesn't need to be any pressure. You are both consenting adults, enjoying each other's company. He'll either get bored and leave you in the dust for a supermodel, or you'll stay together, eventually get pictured in the magazines and lose your job. Win-win situation, right? She scoffed.

Undoing her seatbelt, she turned to get out of her door. A face was right up against the window. She screamed. And then she realised it was Josh. He opened the car door for her, a cheeky grin on his face, his dark hair perfectly styled.

"Sorry, I didn't mean to scare you." He extended his hand to help her out of the car.

Her heart thumped in her chest. Taking his hand, she playfully slapped at his chest. "Don't scare me like that." His lips were wrinkled together, his eyes bright, suppressing the laugh he surely wanted to let escape. "It's not funny."

"Sorry." He kissed her forehead softly and then scanned the street. Was he worried about being seen with her as well? She shoved the thought away, and grabbed her bags.

"I didn't think you were here yet. I couldn't see your car."

"I brought another one." He picked up a bag of food he had placed beside him. "I thought the Aston Martin would be too obvious again. I should have thought about that the other night." Sophie turned from him, hurt that he *was* worried about being seen with her. "I'll grab those for you." He went to take the bags of marking she had to do for the kids' school project about the rainforest.

"No." She twisted them away from his grasp. "I got it."

His eyebrows drew together ever so slightly. "Okay…" He scrutinised her.

Turning from him so he couldn't see her face, she opened her front door for them.

Something was up with Sophie. The way she had pulled away from him when he offered to take the bags for her said it all. Josh followed her into the dining room, her perfume tickling his nose as they walked.

"How was your day?" he asked. He would find out what was wrong—it was just a simple process of elimination.

"Okay, thanks." She shrugged him off, depositing the bags on the small wooden table.

"How was the drive over?"

She turned to him, her eyebrow raised. "Fine." She drew the word out, squinting at him.

He turned around to put his bags in the kitchen, hiding himself from her questioning gaze.

"Thanks for letting me come round again today. I'm sorry I had to leave you this morning." He unpacked the bits from the bags, storing chicken and vegetables in the fridge, along with a bottle of white wine. Sophie didn't say anything. Maybe it was him? "Did you want a glass of wine?" he called out to her.

"Not at the moment," she replied, her tone short.

Yep, it was him.

He poured her a glass of water and went to hand it to her.

"Here you go."

She took the glass from him, avoiding touching his fingers and looking in his eyes.

"What have you and the kids been up to today?"

"We were finishing off their rainforest projects." She pointed to the bags of binders. "We did some P.E. and reading. They had a good day, I think."

"Did you need to do some work? I can entertain myself for a while if you do." He brushed a strand of hair from her face. Maybe she just needed some time to decompress.

"Yeah, that might be good. If you don't mind."

"Of course not. I just want to be around you." He pulled her towards him, unable to help himself. He kissed her, having missed her all morning and afternoon. She pulled away first. "You work as long as you need to. I'll start dinner at five." He kissed her hair and let her go. She needed time. And he needed time to figure out what he'd done.

An hour later, Josh sat on Sophie's sofa, his legs curled underneath him, at ease in her space. Everything about this place made him feel at home. Sophie sat at her table, marking, silent. Something was still up with her, but just being around her had his creative juices flowing and so he sat, writing and humming to himself. Then he looked at his watch. Bugger, it was already five fifteen. Putting aside his pen and paper, he walked over to Sophie.

Bending down, he planted a soft kiss on her hair. "I'm late starting dinner. Do you want anything? A cup of tea, a glass of wine?" He could get used to this.

"I think a glass of wine is in order after all this rainforest knowledge." She sighed, putting her pen down. There were a bunch of stamps sprawled out in front of her, from 'good job', to 'great work' and 'excellent'. Each one had a different animal on them holding up a sign.

Josh pulled out the chair next to her. "Are they doing well?"

"Yes." She shifted the project books around. "They seem to have really engaged with the project. It's nice when the kids who don't have a very stable home life, or are always the ones causing disruptions, produce good work. They've done really well." She couldn't hide her proud smile. Even if she was annoyed with him.

"You really love what you do, don't you?" He stroked her back, glad to see she didn't pull away from his touch.

She nodded. "I really do."

"Are you going to tell me what's wrong yet?"

She sighed and leant back in her chair. "What's going to happen with us?"

"What do you mean?"

"Well, how is this going to work out? Are you really interested in me? Or have I been too easy?"

"Sophie, where is this coming from?" He leant towards her, taking her hand in his. He had no idea where this insecurity was coming from. Maybe from her shitty ex-boyfriend and how he had treated her. He gulped. Or maybe from him leaving her after their first night together.

"I just got to thinking, really how is this going to end?" Pulling her hand from his, she stood and walked to the kitchen.

Josh followed her. "Who says it will end?" Sophie scoffed as she poured herself a glass of wine, so he carried on. "No, seriously, who says it's going to end? I'm not planning on ending it. Are you?" He scrutinised her, trying to read her mind. She shrugged again. His heart seared in pain, as if she had jabbed a knife into it. "Are you thinking of ending it?" He had to know.

"No, but let's be honest here, you aren't going to be spending the rest of your life with little old me, are you?"

He grabbed her hand again and put her glass of wine back down on the counter. "Why wouldn't I? Why do you think I would be the one to leave?"

"Because you already did!"

His stomach hit the floor. She was right. He had left. And

now he had to make up for it, every second of every day. He had broken her trust. Would he ever earn it back?

"Come here." He pulled her towards him but she resisted. "Please, Sophie." Giving in, she went to him and he wrapped his arms around her. "I'm sorry. I'm here to stay." Something stirred in him despite himself, having her body pressed against his. "Let me make you forget," he whispered into her ear, and her body shivered against his.

"How are you going to make me forget?"

"I want to take you upstairs and put those condoms to good use." He sucked her ear lobe, eliciting a little moan from her. "And then I will cook you dinner, and we'll sit and watch TV or a film, or read a book. Whatever you want to do, as long as we're together."

"You're too good with words," she whispered.

"I'm good with something else too." He wiggled his eyebrows at her.

Sophie lazed on Josh's naked body, fully sated, her own body still tingling. Yes, he was so good with words that it almost made her question him, but his actions said it all. That was what she needed to remember, in those dark moments when she was scared this wouldn't work out or that she would lose everything in the process. Josh's actions showed her what she needed to know.

He lay underneath her cheek, his arms wrapped around her, his fingers tapping on her shoulder.

Dum, dum, dum, dum, dimmity da dum dum.

Over and over again.

"What is that tune you're tapping?" She tickled his chest.

"Something new." He carried on tapping. "It's just starting to come to me." Leaning up on her elbow, she looked at him, his eyes still closed, his forehead wrinkled, the tapping not stopping. He opened his eyes and asked, "Do you have a pen and paper up here?"

"Erm, I should do."

"Where is it? I need to write this down."

She made a naked dash to her dressing table and riffled

through the drawers. He started humming, now sitting up, the duvet covering him.

"Here." She handed him the pad and pen, then slid back into bed to cover herself up and watched him write away.

Nodding his head and tapping his foot, he scribbled out words, drumming the pen against the pad, humming and muttering to himself.

Sophie stayed silent, watching him for a while, mesmerised by his working process and seeing the creativity flow from him to the paper. As she watched, she felt privileged to be able to see this side of Josh, his talent literally pouring out of him. This was a side that not everyone saw, not his fans, not the paps. And boy, were they missing out. Josh was lost in his work, his forehead scrunched, his beautiful voice singing soft mutterings of phrases.

"I'll make dinner," she whispered with a smile, kissing his head and getting dressed. Josh was so into his words he barely looked up.

She went about preparing the chicken breasts to sear and roasting the winter vegetables, while Josh made his way downstairs, still lost in his notes and humming. Who knew what he had planned for dinner, or even if he was on some sort of fad, celebrity diet. But seeing as he hadn't looked up from the dining table once, he would have to eat what he was given. He'd apologised when he got downstairs and offered to make dinner, but she had batted him away and told him not to worry about it. She could see his fingers were still tapping out that tune, and so with a smile, she had turned him around and sent him out of her kitchen.

Her mobile phone vibrated in her back pocket. Belle. Closing the kitchen door so she didn't disturb Josh in his flow, she answered with a whisper. "Hiya."

"Hey. Why are you so quiet? Have I caught you at a bad time?"

"No, just don't want to be too loud."

She wasn't sure why, but she didn't want to blurt out to Belle that Josh was in the other room. Seeing how rocky Belle's relationship had been with Scott, and how badly it had gone when she'd met Josh, it was probably best she didn't mention it.

"And why would that be?" Belle prompted.

"No reason."

"You're such a bad liar, do you know that? I'm guessing Josh is there and you think it's best not to tell me so I don't go off on one. But have you thought that maybe if you confided in me you were seeing him, and had had a proper apology from him, *and* told me that he was on his best behaviour and treating you properly, maybe I would be supportive?"

Sophie gulped. "Well, when you put it that way, I just sound silly."

"So he's round for a second night?"

"Uh-huh."

"Why can't you talk? Ew, don't tell me you two are naked in bed."

"No." Sophie giggled. "He's writing and I don't want to disturb him."

"I thought you two would be having date night."

"We are. I'm making dinner."

Hands wrapped around her waist, pulling her in tight, and she relaxed into Josh's arms. He rocked them side to side. His body next to hers sent little tingles of happiness and lust into her tummy.

"Hello, Belle," Josh called out, his ear pressed against the phone as if they were sharing it.

"Josh," Belle replied. Sophie was sure her lips were pursed together the way she did on the rare occasion she tried to hold her tongue.

"Would you like to talk?" Josh asked.

"I think that would be a good idea," Belle replied. "We have some things to air out."

Josh took the phone from Sophie's grasp before she could wrench it away from him. No way did these two need to be talking. Sidestepping Sophie's lunge, Josh winked at her and held the phone to his ear, keeping her at bay with one outstretched hand.

"You carry on making dinner. I have some making up to do." He kissed her forehead tenderly and retreated to the living room.

Sophie bit her lip. She should just march in there and wrench the phone from his hands. Shouldn't she? Or maybe not. Maybe they did need to talk. Josh was a grown man after all, he should be able to handle Belle.

She gulped. She had yet to meet anyone who didn't shy away from Belle's temper.

Turning the chicken, she was glad to see the dark brown griddle lines seared onto the underside. Her tummy rumbled.

If the two of them got on, that would make her life a whole lot easier. It had been hard to navigate her relationship with Scott while Belle had outwardly disliked him so much. There had been no one to speak to when they had an argument, or she questioned their relationship. Having Belle there to help and guide her through all this would make a world of difference. Maybe Belle could even help her talk out all these insecurities that had started to pop up.

She went to set the dining table. She piled up Josh's papers and scribbles to one side, not looking at what he'd written. She didn't want to invade his privacy.

Then she dished out the dinner, pouring them both a glass of white wine. Just as she was finishing bringing out the plates of food, Josh came back in from the living room and handed her the phone.

"Hello?" she said to Belle.

"Well, I like him!" Belle declared. "For now anyway." And she hung up before Sophie could even utter a syllable.

"You really are good with words." Sophie pocketed her phone. Josh wrapped himself around her again, swaying to the incessant music he must always hear.

"Being good with words is part of my job, my calling in life. But it doesn't mean that what I say is lies."

She turned to kiss him lightly on the lips. "Come on, dinner's ready."

Josh took her hand and led her to the table, twirling her as they went. Every time he did that, she felt like a little girl again, as if she had not a care in the world.

"Sorry I left you to make dinner," he said.

"I don't mind. I don't know what you had planned, so I just threw this together."

Josh started to tuck into dinner, moaning at his first bite. "It's delicious. Not quite the date night I was hoping to give you. Sorry about that." He rubbed the back of her hand.

"It was nice seeing you create. It's a side to you I haven't seen. Have you written a whole song?"

He chuckled. "Unfortunately no. It's a long process. It'll take me weeks to eke out every line, and the melody, and then there's layering up different instruments, recording it, changing it. But it's a start at least."

They sat in silence for a while as they ate. "So, what did you say to Belle? She changed her tune on you quite quickly."

Josh gulped down his mouthful, his eyes watering. He took a drink of water. "I just told her the truth. That I'm not trying to mess you around and that I'm trying to make up for the hurt I caused you. And I invited her to lunch at the weekend."

"What?" It was Sophie's turn to swallow her barely chewed mouthful. "You're having lunch with her?" He was either very brave, or very naïve. Belle would rip him apart.

"Is that not okay? I meant it last night when I said I wanted to show your family and friends I care for you. I thought you could invite your brother and Tony, too?"

Yep, naïve. "I don't think you want to do that. It would be like walking into a lion's den."

"Sophie." He put his knife and fork down and reached across to hold her hand. "I meant what I said. I have making up to do, and being open with your loved ones, and getting to know them and letting them know me is one of the steps to do this. And I'm not a wimp, you know? I sing on sold-out world tours, I sit in front of record label executives, I go on live TV to do interviews. I'm sure I can handle three people."

CHAPTER 17

Josh wiped his hands down his jeans. God, he was never normally nervous, but right now his stomach felt like it could rip in two and his palms were so sweaty. He continued pacing up and down the living room, looking out the window for any sign of the lunch guests. Sophie walked in, carrying a tray with some snacks.

"Stop worrying." She put the tray on the coffee table and walked over to him, kissing him gently on the cheek and squeezing his hand. "They will love you."

He scoffed. "You're joking, right? Belle tore me a new one last weekend, John was soaking up every minute of my discomfort and was definitely happy to stick the knife in a bit further, and Tony? Who knows what Tony is going to be like?" He fluffed a cushion on the sofa. He'd probably fluffed that cushion five times already.

"You forgot about Jodie and Max." She giggled, walking away back to the kitchen.

"So you and John both like to stick the knife in?" Josh called to her retreating back.

He blew out a shaky breath.

Returning with a stack of plates, Sophie laughed at him again. "What happened to not being a wimp, and what was it? 'Singing in front of sold-out crowds, and doing live TV interviews'."

"You're enjoying this far too much." He sat on the edge of the sofa, his knee bouncing up and down.

"I like watching you squirm." She sat on the arm of the chair next to him, rubbing his back. "Honestly though, you'll be fine. And I'm here to protect you."

The shrill doorbell rang, piercing his very being. *Fuck.*

Sophie kissed his head. God, now he would never be able to claim he was brave. He stood up, drawing his shoulders back and plastering a smile on his face. Fake it till you make it. He followed Sophie to meet his doom.

Belle stood at the front door, bottle of wine and flowers in hand, smiling brightly.

"Hi!" Sophie hugged her tightly and ushered her through.

"Hi, Belle." Josh kissed her cheek gently and took the wine and flowers from her so he could make a quick retreat to the kitchen. God, what had got into him? He messed around with the flowers, putting them into a vase of water.

"You two are cosy." Belle stood in the doorway, peering in as he arranged the flowers and Sophie poured her a glass of wine.

The doorbell rang again and Sophie left to open it, leaving him with Belle. "Are you still on your best behaviour?" she asked him, sipping from her glass, her eyes never leaving his as she drank.

"I thought you'd changed your mind about me." He turned to her. *Stop being a wimp.*

Belle scrunched up her face. "I decided to give you the benefit of the doubt. Scott was a complete arsehole. I won't let my best friend waste any more of her time on another arsehole, so don't be one."

"Has anyone ever told you that you're scary?"

She laughed, a deep, genuine laugh that filled the kitchen. "People are normally too scared to tell me that. Look, I wear my heart on my sleeve, I say what I think, and I get agitated easily. But…I'm very loyal, and Sophie means the world to me. You treat her right and we will be friends. Believe it or not, I'm not here to make your life difficult."

"Are you causing trouble again, Belle?" She turned around to face a tall man with dark brown hair swept over to one side. This must be Tony. A brown spaniel, the same colour as the man's hair, stood obediently next to him. He bent down to kiss Belle on both cheeks. "I heard that James had to escort you out of the pub last weekend because you were misbehaving."

She screwed up her face again. "Pft, I don't know what he thought he would achieve."

Tony walked past her, a big grin on his face. He held his hand out to Josh and shook it in a firm grip. "Hey, I'm Tony."

"Nice to meet you, Tony. I'm Josh."

"And this is my girlfriend Jodie." He pulled a pretty woman towards him.

"Hi, Jodie." Josh bent to kiss her cheek, careful not to linger.

"Uh, hi," she stuttered, a pink blush spreading across her cheeks.

Yep, she knew exactly who he was and was obviously a bit star-struck. He prayed she could be trusted to not leak anything to the press about him and Sophie. Tony pulled her back to his side.

"And that's Max." Tony pointed to the dog, who was standing patiently in front of Josh, waiting for some attention. Luckily Josh was a dog lover and bent down to greet him, getting a good ear sniff from the charming little dog with tufty hair.

"Where did Soph go?" Belle asked.

"John had just pulled up too, so she's waiting for him," Tony replied.

Josh straightened up, remembering that he was joint host here. "Would you like a drink?"

"I brought some beers, me and Jodie will have one of those, thanks. Just in the bottle is fine."

Josh rummaged through the second drawer for the bottle opener and busied himself with opening the bottles.

"You know your way around the kitchen," Tony added as Josh passed them the open bottles. Jodie nudged him in the ribs. "What?" Tony rubbed them.

"Ignore him," Jodie said. "I warned him to be on his best behaviour."

"Hello, everyone," John called out as he entered the kitchen. The small space was now full to the brim with everyone standing in it. John kissed the ladies on their cheeks and shook hands with Tony and Josh.

Sophie stood in the doorway. "Shall we go into the living room? We'll have a bit more space."

Everyone made to move and Josh held back, letting them all go first. He joined Sophie at the door, and she kissed him on the cheek. "You okay?" she whispered into his ear.

"Yeah. You?" He walked her through the dining room to the living room where everyone was talking and catching up. He felt stronger and braver with her next to him, his initial nerves subsiding. This was important—he had to impress her friends and her brother. If he didn't, she might just end it.

"Yes, I just want you to relax." She laid her hand on his stomach.

"Thanks for having us, Josh and Sophie." John lifted his beer bottle to toast them.

"Don't go easy on him, John," Belle chimed in, her lips curling up at the sides.

"I think we can all go easy on him with you here to make his life difficult," Tony said, leaning across the coffee table to grab some snacks.

"Look." Sophie straightened up, pulling Josh tighter against her, her hand gripping the back of his shirt. "What has happened has happened. I don't want anyone to give Josh a hard time. We have spoken about that weekend, Josh has apologised and we've decided to move forward. We don't need anyone's input on that. You're just here to get to know him, and that's that. Okay?" She pulled her chin up high.

So that was how she was in the classroom, commanding the attention of thirty students. Everyone had turned to look at her, taking in her every word, and now they were all nodding.

"Good." Sophie nodded too. "Well, let's have a nice time then." She bent towards John's bottle and tapped it with her glass, the chime ringing through the room.

"Well then, I suppose we all know where we stand." Belle leant forward to join in on the cheers and the rest of them followed.

Everything seemed to be going well. Josh's palms had returned to an acceptable level of moisture, and his smile wasn't plastered on to cover his nerves. Now it was genuine, smiling at the group around him, Sophie's loved ones. They were a good bunch, constantly joking like he and Sean did. He hoped he was making just as good of an impression on them as they had on him.

"Any more drinks?" Josh offered the room.

"A cup of tea would be lovely." Sophie smiled up at him from her place on the sofa. Josh couldn't help but stroke her cheek. She was happy. That was all that mattered.

"Oh go on then, tea would be great," Belle added, nudging Sophie in the ribs to break up their gaze.

"Coffee for me please," Jodie added.

"I'll help you, Josh." John got up from his chair, walking out to the kitchen before Josh could reassure him that he could manage. Was he in for the 'big brother' chat? Josh's palms grew sweaty again.

"And I'll just let Max out." Tony signalled for Max to follow him and went into the kitchen too.

Yep, he was in for it all right. The nerves he had banished only a couple of hours earlier firmly settled in his stomach.

John was already boiling the kettle when he got to the kitchen.

"Come on then, let me have it." Josh closed the kitchen door behind him so the girls couldn't hear.

"Come on then what?" John lined up three mugs on the counter.

"The big brother chat. The one where you ask me what my intentions are with Sophie. If I'm in it for the long run. The one where you warn me that if I ever hurt her you'll hunt me down and kill me."

John shrugged his shoulders, concentrating on spooning coffee into a mug for Jodie. "Don't know what you're talking about."

Tony leant against the back door, his arms crossed, a slight smile on his lips, his eyes dancing with amusement.

"So you didn't come in here to lecture me?"

"Listen, if I wanted to lecture you, I would tell you to never pull a stunt like that again." John turned an icy-cold stare to Josh, pointing the teaspoon at his face like a gun. "I would tell you that at the tiniest whiff of something dodgy going on that you would regret having ever laid eyes on my sister. I would tell you that every moment of every day you are alive, you are to make up for the hurt you caused her. That you need to treat her with respect and like the princess she deserves to be treated like. I mean it, Josh, I don't care who the fuck you are, you don't mess with her again. You got that?" John raised his eyebrow, his tattooed forearms clenching.

Josh nodded. "I don't need your warning, John. I know I fucked up. It scared me how I felt that night and it freaked me out. That whole week, I tried to stay away, but as soon as I saw her again, I just couldn't turn my back. She'd be better off without me, without this life and all the craziness that surrounds me. But I can't let her go. I tried. I really tried."

"Listen." John walked towards him, slapping him firmly on the arm. "I could see how much you liked her when you walked into the pub. There's something between you. Something so obvious. I saw the same thing between Tony and Jodie, before they could even see it, and I saw it between you and Sophie. Just don't fuck it up." He slapped Josh's arm again for good measure and turned back to pour the boiling water into the mugs, as if nothing had been said.

Tony had stayed in the same position throughout their chat, the corners of his mouth turned up ever so slightly. "Have you told her how you feel?"

Josh shook his head. "I can't, it's too soon."

"That's what I thought with Jodie, and then I almost lost her by getting in my own way. Hurting the one person I never wanted to hurt. I wish I'd told her how I felt the moment I realised, but I didn't. I hid it, squashed it down, rejected it. Time is precious. Don't waste it."

He walked with Max to where Josh was standing by the door, grabbing Jodie's coffee on the way past.

"Show her you're crazy about her, in everything you do. But more importantly, Josh, tell her."

He patted Josh on the back then opened the door and brushed past him into the living room. John followed with

Belle's cup, and another beer for himself. And Josh was left with Sophie's mug, with hearts dotted all over it.

Shit. Did he love her?

Sophie watched Josh bringing her tea in her favourite cup as if he were carrying a china doll. He stared at the drink, treading carefully so as not to spill one drop, his arm out to one side as if he were walking on a tightrope. "Here you are." He handed her the cup, holding onto it for a brief second and gazing intently into her eyes before releasing it.

Sophie looked around at everyone, bewildered by his behaviour. Had he been abducted by aliens or something in the kitchen? As she glanced at the girls, who seemed equally baffled, she caught the knowing looks on John and Tony's faces. What on earth was going on?

"Thanks." She placed the cup on the table, as if it were a bomb.

"Did you have 'the chat' then boys?" Belle asked, dipping a biscuit into her tea.

"We can neither confirm nor deny that a chat took place." John sipped his beer. Tony squeezed Jodie's knee. Josh wouldn't look at Sophie again.

"You didn't, did you?" she pleaded with her brother.

John shrugged, avoiding her gaze.

A clatter of plates sounded loudly. Max had chomped on something from the coffee table. Tony attempted to wrestle with the dog and grab whatever it was that he had stolen from his mouth.

"You little bugger." Tony gave up and wiped his hands on a napkin. "That is well and truly gone. Whatever it was. Naughty boy, Max." Max looked up at him, not one bit ashamed of his behaviour, just perfectly satisfied that he had found a treat. "I'm so sorry, Sophie."

"Oh, don't worry, that sausage roll had been left for a while, it's a surprise he didn't try to nab it earlier. I'll tidy the rest up so he's not tempted." She sat forward, beginning to clear empty plates and gather leftover food.

"I'll do that." Josh took the plates from her, carrying on from where she had stopped.

"I'm happy doing it. And then I can grab the cake."

"No, honestly. You sit back and relax with your friends. I've got this." Josh retreated to the kitchen, carrying everything from the table in one trip.

Sophie wrinkled her face up at Jodie, who just shrugged back. Belle smirked at Tony and John, who were exchanging knowing looks. What on earth had they said to him?

As Tony and John started talking about the pub, Jodie scooted towards her on the sofa and bent her head to whisper, "It all seems to be going really well with you two then, Sophie?"

"Yeah, I think so. I don't even know what this is to be honest, but it's nice. And he's nice. He's spent every night here since Monday."

"Oh, really?" Jodie raised her eyebrows. Max had laid his head on her knee and she was absently stroking him while he looked up at her, love-struck. "Have you not been to his place yet?"

Sophie shook her head, checking towards the kitchen to see if Josh was heading back. "No, not yet. He hasn't even mentioned it. I think because I'm working every day and it's easier for me to travel to work from here, it has just sort of fitted. He's travelled back to London for a few meetings, but he just comes straight back."

"Well, yes, that makes sense, I suppose. When are you

meeting his best friend? John was telling us that Sean was a laugh. We thought he might have been here, actually."

Sophie nibbled her lip. "He hasn't said anything about that. He wanted to meet you guys, but I don't know about Sean. Obviously I met him briefly at the pub, but didn't get to know him well."

Jodie nodded, a strange look on her face, as if she were surprised. Was there something wrong with that? Should she be worried?

Josh returned, cutting their conversation short, handing her the first bowl with a big slice of chocolate cake. He'd had it delivered especially for them in the morning while she went food shopping. "The biggest slice for you." He winked at her and turned to hand Jodie her slice.

Max woke up from Jodie's knee and sniffed at the bowl. "I think that's enough treats for you, Max." Jodie clicked for him to lie down and he obeyed immediately, his eyes still trained on the bowl.

CHAPTER 18

Sophie lay on her bed, exhausted, waiting for Josh to come up. They had not long said goodbye to everyone, and tidied up together in comfortable silence. Then Josh had made her another cup of tea and sent her to bed, smacking her playfully on the bum as she went. He'd wanted to jot down some thoughts before he came up.

She scrolled through her phone mindlessly. They'd had a good day, and everyone seemed to really like Josh. But something that Jodie had hinted at was starting to eat away at her, like a parasite. Eating away at her happiness and souring it to something else.

The bedroom door opened and Josh poked his head in. "I'm just going to jump in the shower. Do you want anything?"

So many things that I can't possibly tell you. "No, I'm alright thanks." He went to close the door. "Josh?" she called after him, and he turned back round. "That went well today, don't you think?"

He smiled down at her, as she was snuggled in bed in her cotton pyjamas. Hardly sexy…maybe she should make more of an effort.

"I think it went really well. I really liked all of them. So hopefully they liked me back."

"Even Belle?"

"Especially Belle." He beamed.

She wasn't used to having her friends and family get on with her boyfriend. Not that Josh was her boyfriend. But it was a strange feeling for them to get on with her…whatever you would call Josh. Lover? She cringed.

"You okay?" He sat on the edge of the bed, taking her hand in his and playing with her fingers.

"Yeah," she chirped, covering up the paranoia that was growing in her. "So when do you want me to meet Sean?"

Josh drew his brows together. "You've already met Sean."

"Yeah, I know, but properly. Like you met all my friends and family."

"Oh." He stared at the wall, thinking. "I hadn't really thought, to be honest."

"Okay." Her heart took a nosedive and a tiny lump rose in her throat. Josh leant forward and kissed her hair before getting up and heading for the door. "And I was thinking," she called to him before he reached it, "we can stay at your place this week if you want? We've been here all week and I'm sure you have bits and pieces to get on with. And it might be nice to be at yours for a while."

He nodded slowly. "Well, I've been staying here so it's easier for you to get to work." He shrugged, fiddling with the door handle.

"I know, but I wouldn't mind driving down for the week if you wanted to." She wrapped a tassel from a cushion around her finger. "It's just a thought." She concentrated on twisting the tassel so tightly around her finger that it made the tip bright white. When she released it, the pink flooded back.

"Okay, well, we'll see how it goes, yeah?"

"Yeah, okay. It's no big deal."

Josh tapped the door and left for his shower.

But it was a big deal. How were they going to progress if he didn't even want to introduce her to his loved ones or even welcome her into his home? The little lump in her throat grew an inch bigger. She didn't even know where he lived. He had just said London.

She picked up her phone. Maybe she could Google it. She opened up the internet page, and began to type in his name.

No.

She threw the phone to the end of the bed as if it were a bomb. She couldn't start going down that route. Who knew what she would uncover or find out that she didn't want to know?

She had to trust him. To trust this. She had to get over these stupid insecurities. When she had met Scott she hadn't been this needy. She needed to chill out. As and when Josh wanted her to go to his house, or meet his friends and family, that would have to be good enough.

And if he never did? She punched her pillow to lie down. Then she would have a hard decision to make.

Josh rinsed off the last of Sophie's body soap. He had brought his own from home, but there was something so comforting about being wrapped in her scent that he just couldn't resist.

He had been practicing in his head, again and again, the words he was going to say to her. Tony was right. He should just tell her. He'd even written bits down before he came upstairs, just to get the jumble of words out of his head and in some order. To try and figure out the best combination of words so that she knew he truly meant it.

Pulling on some shorts to sleep in, he hung his towel over the door and headed to their room. *Sophie's* room. This wasn't his house. Even though, in such a short space of time, it felt like home. Sophie lay in bed on her side, wrapped up in the duvet, both her hands under her cheek as if she were praying, a slight frown on her forehead. She was sound asleep.

He slid under the duvet next to her, pulling her against his chest to snuggle. She hardly roused. And before he knew it, her breathing deepened and she was sound asleep again. But this time, right where she belonged.

He sighed. He had taken so long to plan what he was going to say and how he was going to say it, that by the time he was ready she was fast asleep. *Typical.*

He stroked up and down her back. But Tony was right, he just needed to say it.

Forgetting all the words he'd planned and written down, he just said the three words that mattered. Three words that she couldn't hear. Three words that she wouldn't remember.

"I love you."

CHAPTER 19

Sophie laid down her book as Josh brought in a slice of cake and a cup of tea to the living room. "You're going to make me fat with all this cake and tea."

He scoffed. "As if. You do enough running around after the kids at school to work off those calories." He placed the bowl and mug on the coffee table and sat next to her, pulling her feet up onto his lap.

"Josh, I have had chocolate, or chocolate cake, or chocolate pudding or any other form of chocolate you can imagine, every day you've been staying here." She raised an eyebrow at him, but couldn't resist tucking into a bit of the cake. "I have no willpower to resist."

"That's good to know." Smirking, he started to massage one of her feet.

"Oh wow, I might actually be in heaven." She laid her head back on the cushion behind her.

"From the cake or the massage?"

"From both at the same time. Are you finished with your writing?"

They'd been having a lazy Sunday together, Josh writing

away at her dining table, his guitar placed next to him as usual, while she read in the living room. She loved watching him create. Loved listening to him strumming chords and working through a melody. It all sounded wonderful to her ears, but Josh seemed to think he could improve it. And low and behold, he did every time.

"For now." He concentrated on massaging her foot.

"Did you want to pop to the pub this afternoon? John will be there."

"Erm…" He didn't say anything else.

"We don't have to, I just thought it might be nice to get out of the house for a bit. It's a lovely autumn day. How about we go for a little walk?"

"I think I'd rather stay in." He didn't look at her. "I can get some more writing done."

"Oh, okay."

She put her bowl down, suddenly losing her appetite for chocolate cake. Or anything else for that matter. Did he not want to be seen out with her?

"Well, I might still go. I want a bit of fresh air." She slipped her foot from his fingers, sad that only one foot had received attention. But she needed to get out of here. Away from him. Away from her thoughts.

"Yeah, of course. No problem. I can cook a nice dinner for when you get back."

She stopped putting her coat on to consider him. Too busy writing to go out, but not too busy to make dinner? She pulled her hair out from her coat. "I won't be long. I'll text you when I'm on my way back."

And she left her home without a second glance.

Trudging through the woods hadn't helped. Listening to the autumn leaves fall in the soft wind hadn't helped. Sophie's brain was still fuzzy. Maybe going to the pub would help?

She turned down a lane to walk the short distance to the pub. Her brother would cheer her up. Get her mind off of everything. She pushed open the heavy door and was greeted by the sound of punters talking away with one another, cutlery clinking from the restaurant and the fire crackling in the open fireplace.

John stood behind the bar. She was so used to seeing him here, his sleeves rolled up exposing his tribal tattoos, a tea towel over his shoulder. Just being with him was comfort enough.

He smiled over at her, a big toothy grin, and looked behind her for Josh. His eyebrow went up and stayed up as she leant against the bar.

"He's writing," she explained. "Can I have a large glass of white wine, please?" John didn't move. "I'm not driving, don't worry." Not saying a word, he moved to pour her a glass.

Placing the glass in front of her, he held it so she couldn't take a sip. She looked up into his caring eyes and saw his forehead was wrinkled with concern.

"Soph, I've worked in pubs all my working life. I know the look of someone drinking in pain or to forget troubles. I'm here to talk. But I don't think you need me." He turned to look up the other end of the bar. "Jodie!" he shouted. Jodie popped her head round the bar behind a group of customers. Sophie hadn't seen her perched on the bar stool. "Sophie needs you." He knocked on the bar and left to serve more punters.

Jodie waved her over, tapping a bar stool next to her that was empty. Sophie wound her way through everyone and kissed Jodie on the cheek, then stroked Max's head. "I didn't see you over here. You okay?"

"Yeah, you? Tony is just checking over the restaurant and

then we're heading home for a stew. Where's Josh?" She looked around.

"At home. He wanted to get some writing done." Sophie shrugged off her winter coat, hanging it on a little hook underneath the bar top. The fire crackled behind her, warming her back.

"What's going on? You look all brooding." Jodie sipped her Coke. Sophie shrugged, not knowing where to begin. Or even if she should. "Come on, Tony will be back in a minute. Give me all the details."

"I don't know. You just got me thinking yesterday. Josh is becoming part of my world, but I'm not a part of his."

"And you want to be?"

"Yes. I mean I don't want to be followed by the paparazzi again. That was horrible. And it scares me thinking that's what Josh has to endure. And who knows what will happen with my job if I do pop up in a paper again? They were so annoyed about that first picture. So it does worry me. But I still want to know his friends and family. To see his home." She twirled her glass around and around. "I don't know. I feel so conflicted. I'm not used to feeling like this."

"I think you just need to tell him, to talk to him."

"I asked him last night about meeting Sean properly and suggested staying at his home this week."

"And?"

"He just brushed it off."

"Brushed it off how?"

"He said he hadn't thought about me meeting Sean properly, as we met before. And he said we'd see how it goes with me staying at his this week. But he hasn't mentioned it again."

"Okay, so I think you just need to be open with him and tell him you want to be a part of his world, and it would mean a lot to you. Then if he pushes back any more, you might have a problem. But he seemed really into you yesterday. So, I don't think you will. Tony said he's smitten with you."

Sophie scoffed, her cheeks ablaze. "I don't think Tony has ever said 'smitten' in his life."

"Well, no. But he's really into you. Tony wouldn't tell me exactly what was said. But he likes you. So, give him a chance to prove that. But be honest with him. I bet you brushed off staying at his and meeting his friends as if it wasn't really important?"

Sophie ran through their conversation in her head, and wrinkled her nose up. "I may have said it wasn't a big deal."

Jodie chuckled. "See. You haven't even given him a chance."

Tony appeared by Jodie's side, kissing her cheek. "You alright, Sophie? Josh not with you?"

"He's writing," Jodie replied on her behalf.

Thank God for girlfriends. She was getting bored of repeating herself. For years she had turned up without Scott and no one had batted an eyelid. Actually, they probably preferred it. But with Josh, it was different. But then again, everything was different with Josh.

All of a sudden her heart hurt. She had an uncontrollable urge to go home and wrap herself up in the man she cared so much about.

"Everything alright with the restaurant?" Jodie asked Tony.

"Yep, all going smoothly."

"As it usually does. I'll finish this and we can head home, yeah?" Jodie stared up at him, love sparkling in her eyes. Jodie was a natural beauty. She wore no make-up today, her brown curly hair pulled back into a lazy ponytail. Sophie hadn't noticed it before, being too consumed with herself, but Jodie looked tired.

"Of course, my love." Tony pulled her into him so she could lie against his chest.

"How's your business going? Any exciting projects?" Sophie asked her.

"Really good. I'm really busy with the designs for the house builders. They liked them so much that they've given me all the homes to design. And on top of that, I've taken on more clients. And we're thinking about setting up my cottage as a little holiday let."

"Well, that's a lot going on. All sounds great though."

"Yep, but exhausting." Jodie stifled a yawn.

"Come on, let's get you home. You can have a sleep and I'll cook dinner." Tony took her hand.

"I'll walk out with you. I'm heading home too." Sophie drained the last of her wine and signalled to John that she was leaving.

"Are you feeling better?" he asked her, leaning over the bar and giving her a kiss on the cheek.

"Yes, much. Thanks, John."

"Good. Tell Josh I said hi."

"Will do. See you soon."

She followed Tony and Jodie to the door of the pub and Tony held it open for her to go through. "Are you walking home?"

"Yeah, I took a walk through the woods and ended up here."

"Do you want me to see you back?"

"No, it's not long. I'll be okay. You go and look after Jodie."

Jodie pulled her in for a hug and whispered, "Give him a chance."

CHAPTER 20

"Hello?" Sophie called again through the silent hallway. It was deadly quiet. Where on earth was he? "Josh?" she called upstairs, listening out for any movement. Nothing. Maybe he was cooking. She checked the kitchen. Nope. Then she tried the living room.

He lay stretched out on the sofa, headphones in, fast asleep. That peaceful look on his face—the one where he looked like he was happy and content, his lips slightly lifted at the corners —sent her heart melting. He seemed so comfortable here.

Not wanting to disturb him, she settled herself at the dining table to do some marking. Pulling out some of her pupils' exercise books with this week's project, she pushed aside pages and pages of Josh's notes, scribbles, pens and Post-it notes. You name it, it was here, as if a stationery cupboard had been emptied onto her dining table. Normally the table was spotless, but since Josh arrived it had been gradually getting more and more cluttered. He was a messy creator.

Finally sure that there was no organisation to this madness and that Josh would have no clue if she were to move anything out of place, she gathered the papers and put them into piles.

She had refrained from looking at them before now as she didn't know if she was allowed to read anything or not. But her name on a piece of paper caught her eye and she couldn't help but look at it.

'Sophie' was written in his scrawly handwriting, barely legible, surrounded by little doodles of swirls and arrows, crosses and shapes. All around her name were different words. Happiness. Content. Free. Smiles. Laughter. Hope. Beginnings. Different. Memories.

She stared at all the words. Were they about her? Was this a mind map of what he thought and felt about her? Unable to resist, she reached out for another piece of paper and read the short passage scrawled across it.

As she read, her heart filled up with every word that was written, tears falling down her cheeks and staining the page. It was the most beautiful thing she had ever seen.

Second nature made her pull out her marking materials and take out her favourite stamp, the purple ink pad drying out from being used so often. She stamped the corner of the paper and started writing. Then she shoved it into the bottom of the pile and pushed the other papers away. She didn't need to read any more.

Looking through the door to the living room, she saw Josh still sprawled out, his hands behind his head, his breathing deep. Content.

Josh awoke with a start. He never had naps, but he had lain on the sofa, stretching his legs in front of him, and gradually sunk lower and lower, nodding away to his playlist. And before he knew it, he'd been asleep.

He pulled the buds from his ears, the music still playing. He turned his head at movement in the corner of his eye.

Sophie was sitting at the dining table with her head bent low over a piece of work, writing notes. She sat back in her chair, a little smile on her face, the one that always appeared when she spoke about how proud she was of a child that day at school.

She turned her head to look at him, and her smile widened when she saw he was awake. "Hello, sleepyhead."

"How long have you been home?" He stretched out his aching back. He would pay for sleeping on the sofa.

She checked her phone. "An hour."

"I didn't hear you come in. Sorry."

"I'm not surprised, with how loud your music was. How can you sleep with that on?" She pulled the next lot of work towards her.

"I don't normally nap. I must've just drifted off." He noticed the pile of papers at the other end of the table. She had tidied up his work. His heart froze mid beat. "Sorry about all the mess." He went to the table and gathered the papers. Had she seen anything? She must have done—if she'd moved them she would have surely spotted something. Why hadn't he done it himself?

"It's fine." She didn't look up from the paper she was marking, her green pen poised to write. "I just moved them to one side. I hope you don't mind."

He scanned her face. If she had seen anything, surely she would say something, or at least look guilty right now. Or even look like she was hiding looking guilty. His shoulders dropped. Only slightly. "It's your dining table. I shouldn't leave them out. I'll try to keep them a bit neater for you."

"I like that you feel comfortable enough to create here."

She lifted her head at last, letting him gaze into her crystal-blue eyes. How were they always so bright?

"I need to talk to you," she said.

She kicked out a chair for him to sit down on. His heart

seized again. Nothing good ever came after 'I need to talk.' He pulled the chair out further, the legs scraping on the stripped wooden floor, and sat down.

"Am I in your bad books?" He leant forward, his elbows resting on the table. She had left so quickly for her walk, he must have done something to upset her. But what?

"No." She shook her head, fiddling with her pen. "But you were."

He gulped. "What do you mean?" he croaked.

"I needed to get out and get some fresh air to clear my head. And I ended up at the pub and Jodie was there."

He tried to piece together what she was saying. Where was this going? "Okay…"

"I know we haven't defined exactly what this is between us." He opened his mouth to answer but she cut across him. "And I'm not asking you to. But I feel like you've come into my life and you know virtually everything there is to know about me." She sighed. "But last night, I asked whether I could get to know you in a similar way. Meet some of the people you care about the most. Visit your home, to see where you live and write. But it was clear you don't think about opening that world up to me. And then you didn't want to come today, to just take a little walk or go see my brother at the pub. And I don't get it. I need to understand it, Josh. And I need you to be honest with me. If this isn't going anywhere, then I would like to know now."

He was stunned into silence, his mouth gaping like a fish as he tried to find the words he needed to say. The longer he stayed silent, the more her eyes glazed with tears.

"Sophie." He reached across the table for her hand. "If I didn't want to be here I wouldn't be. We had already finished after that first night together. Think about it. If I didn't want to be with you, I wouldn't have asked to see you again for a date, I wouldn't have stayed, and I wouldn't have kept coming back to you. You have to start trusting me, Sophie, trusting us. And last night when you asked about meeting Sean…well, I just hadn't thought about it because you've already met him. But I don't not want you to meet him. If that makes sense. And if you want to see him again then I'll sort something." He squeezed her hand, hoping that would placate her enough.

"And going to yours?" She looked up at him through her long lashes.

"I said we could see how it goes." He shrugged. "It doesn't make a lot of sense for you to stay at mine when you work so close to here. Why go all the way into London to have to drive to work so early in the morning?" He let go of her hand.

The truth was, he didn't want to know how she would react seeing his home. How she would take the sleek designer furniture, the expensive art on the walls he'd been advised to buy for an investment, the paparazzi outside. As much as he wanted to share his life with her, he knew he lived in this crazy, fantasy world. One that people couldn't even begin to comprehend.

He had so eagerly introduced Emily into that world. And that had ended in disaster. The moment she realised how rich he was, everything had changed, and a demon had grown inside her that almost destroyed her.

"Okay, so maybe not every night. But one? One would be fine." She doodled on a notepad placed next to her.

"What about the paparazzi?" It would be so much easier if they just stayed here, kept their relationship here. That way he wouldn't have to ever find out if his money meant more to her than he did. But he knew that couldn't wait forever. At some point he'd have to find out. And he was scared to his very core.

Sophie looked up at him quickly, her eyes wide, her pen still. "Are they there at your house then?" He nodded, assessing every movement, trying to read her mind. "All the time?" she asked, gulping.

"Virtually." There was no twinkle in her eye. He could tell that the thought of being in the paper again wasn't appealing to her. It was repulsive. "I didn't think you wanted to be in the paper again because you could lose your job?" He had to push this—he had to figure out exactly what the driving force was for her to see his house. He'd been blind to what Emily had really wanted. He couldn't make the same mistake twice.

She blanched, her skin turning ashen. "I didn't. I don't." She piled up the marking, tidying her space. "I didn't think they'd be there all the time."

She got up from the table, taking her empty glass with her to the kitchen. She was pulling away from him. Distancing herself physically and emotionally.

He jumped up from the table too and followed her. She couldn't just leave. His heart already ached at the thought.

"Sophie." He pulled her into a hug. "We'll sort something."

"How?" The word was muffled in his chest.

"I don't know, but we will."

He was so fucking screwed.

Sophie slowed on the road, the sky darkening outside and the streetlights just starting to glow. Large, luxurious, Edwardian homes surrounded her. Nerves bubbled in her as she gripped the steering wheel. They had a plan.

After talking and talking and talking, they had finally agreed. She was desperate to see Josh's home, to feel like he wanted her in his life and that she wasn't just some plaything to be kept in the shadows as his dirty little secret. But she couldn't yet risk being pictured with him.

He had been adamant that there would be photographers posted at his home. She couldn't believe it—or more like she didn't want to believe it. But as she drove past number eleven, she saw with her own eyes a handful of men posted there, cameras draped around their necks, takeaway coffee cups in hand. Waiting.

She pulled up and parked along the road, checking in her mirrors that none of the paparazzi had spotted her. Following the plan, she texted Josh, *Here.*

The plan was for Josh to leave his home and lure them away on a short walk around the block, giving her time to sneak in using a spare key he'd given her. She clutched onto her overnight bag and opened her door slightly, ready to move at any minute.

Josh walked out of his front door and jogged down his steps. "Alright?" he called to the photographers, who suddenly stood to attention and started snapping away. "Honestly, guys, I'm just going to the shop."

"Where've you been, Josh?" one asked, following him up the road in the opposite direction from where Sophie was parked. She got out of the car.

"Yeah, you haven't been home for ages," another called out, diverting round a parked car to get in front of him to take a picture.

Sophie quickly ducked down to pretend to tie her shoelace, letting her hair fall in front of her face. The photographer snapped away and then stopped to look through the pictures, allowing Josh to pass him. He started following again, trying to get more pictures.

Sophie waited a little longer, until she couldn't hear their probing questions and it wasn't so obvious she was about to walk into his house. Then, clutching the key Josh had given her, she ran up his steps and unlocked his door, stepped through, and closed it with a *bang* quickly behind her. She blew out her breath, feeling like a criminal, her heart pounding in her chest. Running around and hiding like this was not her cup of tea.

Looking around, she inspected his hallway. Beautiful checked tiles spanned the length of the hall, and tall white walls rose up either side of her. She placed her keys with Josh's on the console table and walked through to the back of the house. Not a thing was out of place, or out on show if it didn't need to be. There wasn't even a coat on the bannister.

At the back was a large kitchen, looking shiny and new like it had never been used, with dark navy cabinets and a granite worktop. A large breakfast island jutted out into a chill-out area that had a sleek leather sofa and a fire. The back wall had been knocked out in favour of large panes of glass looking onto a perfectly manicured lawn.

She stared around the space, in awe to finally see where Josh lived, to see who he really was. She placed her overnight bag at the end of the kitchen island, feeling the sleek countertops. Suddenly she felt so small and insignificant, stupidly only now really realising that Josh Heart was a celebrity, that this was the lifestyle he was accustomed to. And she was suddenly embarrassed she had even invited him into her home. Her tiny little home with its crooked, creaky floorboards, its mismatched furniture, and the kitchen drawers that you had to slam shut to make sure they were fully closed.

Tea. That was what she needed now, to warm her bones and give her some comfort. She looked around the kitchen. Where was the kettle? A fancy coffee machine was built into one of the cupboards, but no kettle stood on the counter. Actually, where was his toaster? She turned this way and that. Surely she was missing something. Who lived without a kettle or a toaster?

The kitchen counters were clear, so she opened a few cabinets. One held dishes, stacked neatly on their sides in a plate rack. Another had rows and rows of glasses—wine glasses, Champagne flutes, tumblers, shot glasses and everything in between. The largest cupboard held boxes, cans and containers of all sizes, all the food neatly stacked or poured into a labelled container. Everything had a place.

But there was no kettle.

Giving up, she perched on a bar stool facing the garden, looking at the tiny white lights illuminating shrubs and bushes. She waited for Josh to return, her knee bouncing up and down on the bottom rung of the stool.

Eventually, the front door clicked open and closed, and footsteps neared the kitchen. Josh turned the corner and strode to her in three quick strides, putting a bottle on the counter before wrapping his arms around her, squeezing her tight. "I'm sorry, that was crazy. Are you okay?" He pulled away from her, holding her cheeks with his cold hands and kissing her forehead.

She nodded, blushing at his attention. "It's fine." She pulled his hands away from her face.

"You look pale. I brought wine from the shop." He picked up the bottle from the counter.

"I was trying to make a cup of tea, but I can't find a kettle."

He looked around, as if also searching for the kettle. Then he turned back to her, smiling, and kissed her cheek. "I'll make you a tea."

He pulled open a cabinet with cups and canisters of tea, coffee and sugar. Placing a tea bag in the cup, he turned to the sink and turned on a thin tap. Water poured out of it, steaming. "Hot water tap." He winked at her.

She wrinkled her nose. "So you actually don't have a kettle? That's so weird. I don't think I like that. It won't be the same."

He stirred in some milk and squeezed out the tea bag. "It's exactly the same. Without the three-minute wait for the water to boil. Or realising halfway through pouring out your cup that you didn't put enough water in the kettle." He placed the cup in front of her. "Trust me, it tastes exactly the same."

"I'm still not convinced." She inspected the cup with soft brown liquid inside. "It has bubbles in it."

"They go. Come on, let me show you around." He grabbed her hand. "Bring your cup."

He took her out to the patio, rolling back one of the large glass panes, the cold air whooshing in.

"It's a lovely big garden," she said, nursing her tea. She was too nervous to take a sip yet, certain it would taste strange.

"Not too bad for London. It's great in the summer, I can open this wall right up."

She nodded. "Everything is very…clean." She didn't know what else to say. The space felt strange and different. It didn't feel like Josh. Her home felt more like Josh than this did.

"I'm a bit of a neat freak," he admitted, closing the door and showing her through to the front snug room.

She scoffed. He was joking, right? "Have you seen the pile of writing on my dining table? I wouldn't call you a neat freak." She looked around the room, with its dark walls and velvet sofas. The shutters were slanted to stop the paparazzi from seeing in, but even so, she stayed in the doorway.

Then Josh walked her upstairs, each board creaking loudly underfoot. At least there was something not so perfect about his home. "That's writing," he said. "I'm all over the place when I'm writing. But everything else I'm neat with." He showed her through the luxurious guest rooms and bathrooms, each larger than the one before, each more swanky, with huge works of art hung on the wall and en-suites with roll-top baths.

God, he must hate staying in her poky two-bedroom house.

She followed him up to the third floor.

"This is my studio space." He let her through and then went to sit at the piano, watching her.

This felt like Josh—the room seemed to vibrate around her, she could feel his energy. Papers were strewn everywhere and instruments littered the space. And then to the side of the room, there was a unit holding awards and pictures of all his achievements.

She walked over and searched through them all. "Well, someone seems to think you're good at what you do." She turned around, pointing back at the cabinet and pulling a funny face.

Josh laughed with her. "I guess." He slapped his thighs, standing up. "Master bedroom next."

She followed him through to the room next door. It took up the whole length of the house. A stunning large bed sat in the middle, littered with large pillows and throws. Off to the side there was a walk-in wardrobe and bathroom.

Sitting on the bed, he placed her overnight bag next to him, watching every move she made again. She took her cup of tea to the back window, looking out onto his long back garden. Just in front of the window was a sofa set and coffee table. She sat down, thinking. What would it be like to live in a place like this? Josh was still studying her carefully.

"Why do you have so many bedrooms for just you?" she asked.

He shrugged and walked over to sit opposite her, lounging back on the sofa, utterly at ease. Sophie however, felt on edge.

"Why buy a poky flat when I don't need to?"

She wrinkled her forehead at him. "It must be a nightmare to clean." She sipped her tea, thankful that it did taste like normal.

"I have cleaners come round."

She gulped. "Of course." How differently they lived. "I'm surprised you want to leave this place." Insecurity started to nibble away at her.

"Sophie, it's just bricks and mortar. It's an investment if anything. Just like the art on the walls." He shrugged again. "Did you not want to see my wardrobe? Women normally go crazy for a walk-in wardrobe." He scrutinised her, watching intently for her reaction.

"No." She shook her head.

"You haven't even seen the basement."

"There's a basement too?" Her tummy churned. How much had this place cost?

"It has my gym and a home theatre."

She stared at him. This flashy side was so unlike the Josh she had known over the past week. She had almost forgotten he was famous, that he had money. But now, being in his space, every single room reminded her. Every piece of furniture, every trinket, screamed money. She longed for her little house with her cluttered sideboards, the mantelpiece with her picture frames, the coffee table you could put your feet up on.

"I'm sure there will be enough time to see that later." She clutched her cup of tea in front of her for comfort. This little cup probably cost more than all her cups and glasses and plates and bowls combined. She set it down on the glass coffee table, ensuring it was on a marble coaster.

What if she broke something? She wouldn't be able to afford to replace it.

"What's going on?" Josh asked quietly, coming round to sit next to her on the sofa. He pulled her into him and wrapped his arms around her.

"It's a bit too much," she whispered into his chest. The thudding of his heartbeat against her cheek calmed her. She breathed him in, his scent so familiar and comforting to her.

This was Josh. *Her* Josh. A big house and expensive furniture didn't change that.

Clinging onto his shirt, she said, "It's a bit daunting how differently we live. I don't know what I pictured, but I didn't picture this."

"Are you wanting to go home?" he whispered into her hair, his voice rumbling deep within his chest.

She shook her head. She needed to stay. "No, I just need you."

"You've got me." He stroked her hair, twirling it around his fingers.

After a long while of sitting and being with each other in silence, Josh's tummy growled.

"You're hungry." She sat up, her hands still resting on his abs. She was anything but.

"I skipped lunch." He still held a lock of her hair in between his fingers. "I'll order some food in." He grabbed his phone. "What do you fancy?"

She shrugged. "I'll go with anything you want. I won't eat a lot."

He furrowed his brows at her, and then turned his attention to his phone, tapping away.

"Let's grab some wine," he said when he'd finished ordering the food. He pulled her against him for a tight hug, then stood up and held out his hand.

Josh dished out portions of rice and noodles, beef and chicken from the Chinese takeout cartons. Sophie stared out into the dark garden lit by lights along the borders. She wasn't herself—she was quiet and brooding.

He'd tried to stay light-hearted, but her sombre mood had seeped into him too. Not for the first time, he wished he wasn't famous. Maybe he needed to step away from this life—he didn't enjoy it anymore anyway. Sure, he would miss the writing and creating a song in the studio. But everything else? He wouldn't miss it at all.

"Here you go, eat up." He handed Sophie her plate.

"I won't eat that much." She stared at the pile of food.

He kissed her head on the way past to take a seat opposite her. "Eat what you can. I haven't got used to dishing out for your tiny appetite yet."

"Just do half of yours." She smiled at him, the first smile since being in his home that didn't also have a shadow behind it. "Apart from the noodles," she added. "I love noodles." She twisted them around her fork and started eating.

"Shall we go back to yours tomorrow?" He concentrated on his plate.

She put her cutlery down, and took a sip of wine. "I'll leave that decision up to you."

"Well, you don't feel comfortable here. And it's easier to be at yours for you." He'd known this was a bad idea. But he also couldn't refuse her. He hadn't expected her to be so turned off by it all. It was completely different to how Emily had reacted. But it was hardly any better. His lifestyle just caused issues. In every single way.

"Did you feel comfortable at mine when you first stayed?"

He nodded, pushing his rice around. "I did."

"I'm trying, Josh." She reached across the counter and entwined their fingers, only just managing to reach him across the wide countertop.

"I know. This is what I was trying to protect you from. I know the world I live in is strange. There's no privacy. No boundaries. I've grown used to it in some respects. I don't expect you to." A part of him didn't want her to get used to it. If she did, would she start changing like Emily had and start craving the limelight?

"I'm sure I'll get used to it. I'll have to, won't I?" She took her fingers back.

Josh rubbed his fingers on a napkin. "What if I stop? What if I give up writing and singing?" He scrutinised her reaction.

She narrowed her eyes at him. "You don't really want to do that, do you? This is your life, your passion. Don't give up anything for me—you'll just come to resent me."

"I wouldn't resent you."

"Of course you would. What, you'd just sit around in your pants all day at mine, while I go out and work?" She shook her head at him.

He shrugged his shoulders. "I wouldn't have to be in my pants."

"What if I lose my job because my face has popped up in the papers again? I thought you could support me." She giggled.

But while she joked, Josh's heart tightened. Is that what she wanted him for? People could so easily hide their true intentions. Is that what she was doing?

"Hey," she called to him, grabbing his attention as his mind wandered away from him. "I'm joking, Josh. I don't want you to support me. My job is more than a job for me. I can't imagine not teaching children. I thought you felt the same way about your work."

"Sorry, I don't know what's got into me." It was like a big black hole had swallowed him up and spat out a miserable version of himself. He put his fork down and placed his napkin on the worktop.

Sophie walked around the counter to him, wrapping her arms around his shoulders. "I do—me. I'm sorry. This isn't how I wanted this night to go. I was so excited to be here. And I am. It's just all this other rubbish has got in the way." She swished her arms around her head. "So let's forget about all of that. And let's just focus on what matters. Us."

She nuzzled his nose. All he could see were her bright blue eyes as his hands cupped her pert bottom.

"Us," he whispered. How amazing that just a few words could change everything—make everything right again. He brought his hand up to her chin. "You're amazing, Sophie."

He kissed her gently, tasting the sweet and sour flavours on her lips. She swiped her tongue around his, just as eager as he was. She wanted him. And he needed her.

He pulled her towards the stairs. "Let's skip dinner."

"But you were hungry." She giggled, pretending to resist, but her feet were walking eagerly despite her hand tugging in his.

"I'm not anymore. And besides, that can wait. You can't."

He twisted her around and caught her in his arms. Her eyes widened, her irises losing the blue, becoming black.

He pushed her against the bannister and bit at her neck, making her draw in her breath. Trailing his hand up her sides, he cupped her breast, brushing her nipple under her clothes. She shuddered beneath him. He flashed her a wicked smile. He loved seeing how she reacted to his touch.

Her eyes lit with defiance and for payback she groped his bulge under his trousers. He sucked in his breath. "I want you in my bed," he growled, the need growing within him.

"I was going. You were the one who stopped me." She pushed him away and sprinted up the stairs in front of him, giggling as he tried to catch up with her.

He caught up with her on the first landing. Grabbing her hips, he pulled her against him. "Not so fast. Let's make it a fair race. And let's make it interesting," he whispered into her ear, cupping her breasts. He just couldn't get enough. She whimpered, rubbing her body against his. "Whoever wins gets to be in charge."

"Deal!" she shouted and launched herself forward, trying to cheat again. But he held her hips and pulled her back, tutting in her ear.

"You're too predictable." He quickly spun her around to face him. "On your marks." He kissed her. "Get set." He cupped her breasts again, making her moan as he sucked her ear lobe. "Go," he whispered and pushed her to the side so he could get around her and start scaling the last set of stairs.

As he sprinted for his life up the stairs, he was sure she must just be behind him, ready to catch up at any moment. But as he was about to turn to cross the landing to get to his door, he stopped. At the bottom of the steps, Sophie stood in her underwear. Matching black, lacy underwear. Her nipples visible through the thin fabric.

He wandered like a zombie back to the top of the stairs

and she started to climb them to join him. Her breasts bounced with every step she took. "How did you get undressed so quickly?" He gulped.

"I ripped my clothes off." She fluttered her eyelashes at him. He didn't move as she got closer. And when she reached the top step, she had to slide her body along his to join him on the landing. She pushed him backwards.

His back thudded against the wall. She reached her hands behind her and fiddled with the clasp on her bra. Releasing it, she dropped the bra onto the floor. He went to step forward, to take a nipple in his mouth.

But she pushed him back again. "Easy, tiger."

Turning on the spot, she placed her thumbs into the sides of the thong that rode high on her hips. Shimmying, she dropped it onto the floor, so that she was stark naked in front of him. Incredible.

Shooting him an evil look over her shoulder, she shouted, "I'm going to win." Then she sprinted, stark, butt naked, into his bedroom, squealing with delight.

He shot after her, captivated by her butt cheeks. Just as she touched the bed, he grabbed her arm and spun her round. They collapsed on the bed together, sinking into the fluffy duvet.

"You cheated." He breathed heavily as Sophie's warm body lay on top of his. "Three times."

"Twice." She pushed up to straddle him. "There wasn't anything in the rules about getting naked." She ground her hips over him. "Josh," she groaned.

He smiled up at her. "Looks like you're paying for your own dishonest behaviour." He lifted his hips slightly so that his bulge rubbed against her more.

"You need to be naked," she told him.

He flipped her onto her back, making her shriek and cling onto his shoulders. He tugged his shirt off and pulled down his trousers and pants in one. He had never undressed so quickly.

"Condom," she moaned. He reached over to the bedside table and grabbed a foil packet. "Here, now," she instructed him urgently.

He pounced back on her, kissing her roughly, making sure his hands didn't move from where they gripped the bedsheet.

"Play with me," she groaned, her voice barely a whisper.

She was a pure vixen lying there, sprawled out on his bed. He had never felt so protective in his life. Never felt such a carnal desire to claim someone as his before.

"How?" he croaked, his mouth dry. She had won unfairly, so there was no way he'd play fairly either. She was about to regret cheating.

"Just touch me." She pulled at his hands to move.

"How?"

He nuzzled her nose and she pulled his head down to her breast. He couldn't resist and licked the sweet nub, making her shiver beneath him.

Picking up one of his hands, she brought it down to her slick centre. Agonisingly slowly, he slid his fingers inside her as his tongue explored her nipple. Her breathing grew quicker. She writhed beneath him as his fingers teased her. Moments later she screamed his name and pulsed through her orgasm.

Without waiting to catch her breath, she wrenched his fingers out of her and pushed him up so that he knelt in front of her. She lowered her head onto him, licking his shaft from base to tip. It was his turn to shudder.

"Sophie," he groaned, desperately trying to not thrust forward. She held onto his hips, not stopping her movement. "Sophie," he pleaded louder. "This is about you." He moved her head away from him.

"This *is* about me. I want to make you come the way you

make me." And she lowered her mouth onto him again before he could protest.

He closed his eyes. If he looked at her, he would erupt. She sped up her movements, her groans vibrating through him. Opening his eyes wide, he looked down at her. Fuck, she was incredible. And now he was so close to coming.

Shit. He wrenched her head from him again and pushed her back onto the bed. Before she realised what he was doing, he hoisted her leg over his shoulder and entered her, pushing quick and hard, thrusting in and out. She bit down on her lip. Faster and faster he thrust, her hips matching his.

"Josh!" she screamed, her head dropping back. He felt her clutch around him, and just as she did, he followed her too. Crashing down on top of her body, slick with sweat, he felt her ragged breathing lifting his body with every breath she took, her heart hammering in her chest against his cheek.

After her breath calmed, she ran her fingers through his hair. "I think we needed that," she whispered, with a quiet giggle. "You would think we hadn't had sex in ages, the way we go at it."

He laughed with her. "I can't get enough of you, that's why." He lifted up from her, something crinkling under his hand. He picked it up. A little square, foil packet. *Fuck.* The condom packet—unused.

He stared in horror at the unopened packet. How the fuck could he have forgotten? It had been on the bed this whole time. "Shit, Sophie." She stared at the packet too. He scooted away from her. "Why the fuck didn't I put it on?" Panic seized his heart. He had never had unprotected sex. Never.

"Whoa, whoa, whoa." Sophie came towards him, her hands held out to calm him. "Josh." She turned his head to look at her. "I'm on the pill. And I've never had unprotected sex."

His chest eased slightly from the suffocating grip wrapped around him. He held her against him, and kissed the top of her head. "God, I'm sorry. I don't know what gets into me when I'm around you. I lost all my senses." He pulled the cover back and settled her in bed with him.

As he lay next to her, he saw that she was biting her lip. "Hey." He pulled it from her teeth. "What are you worrying about?"

"Well, are you clean?" She didn't look at him, but smoothed out the duvet with her fingers.

"Yes." He brushed some hair away from her face. He didn't want to go into the details of always using condoms with anyone he slept with, or getting medically checked. Hopefully that one word was enough from him.

She nodded, her frown easing, and snuggled into his chest. "I think maybe we should just spend all our time together naked and in bed." She traced lines into his chest. "It's easier to concentrate on just us when we're like this. None of that other stuff gets in the way."

"I like the sound of that." He moved some more, getting comfortable. All that other stuff did get in the way. The press, his money and fame, her ex, his ex. But none of it mattered when they were like this.

Sophie twirled more cold noodles onto her fork. She was so ravenous that she couldn't even be bothered to reheat her food. Josh, however, was reheating his in a pan, staring at her with a smile on his face. "You said you weren't very hungry."

"That," she said, chewing her food quickly, "was before you made me run up three flights of stairs and had your dirty way with me."

He laughed. "I think it was the other way round, but whatever." He poured his steaming food back onto his plate and joined her at the counter again.

"I think we should stay here tomorrow night too."

He looked up, his eyes searching hers before he responded. "I didn't think you felt comfortable here."

"Well, the more time I spend here, the more I will feel comfortable. I meant it when I said I want to be a part of your world. It won't be easy with the long drive and all of the guys out there." She pointed her fork towards the front of the house where she was sure paparazzi still sat waiting. "But I think it's important to try."

Josh nodded. "Okay, well, we'll take it one day at a time. Easy breezy."

~

Sophie sat in her car again for the third night in a row, waiting for Josh to leave the house and lure the paparazzi away. She was tired and cranky. It had been a long day at school. The kids had been a handful all day and she just wanted to climb into a hot bath and then lie in her bed watching a film. But instead, she'd had to pack another overnight bag and drive an hour and a half to get to Josh. Only to have to wait another ten minutes in her car for him to leave the house.

Staying at his place every night this week had been her idea. Josh had constantly voiced his concerns that it was too much, that he didn't like the thought of her driving all that way, that he hated having to hide their relationship. And now she agreed with him and wished she hadn't insisted on spending another night here.

He left the house as usual and she waited a bit longer to make sure they were out of sight. As they had every other night, the group of men followed him, taking his picture, shouting questions at him. She sighed. Why hadn't she fallen for someone normal?

She let herself into the empty house. She missed Josh greeting her when she got home. This sucked. She walked straight through to the kitchen and poured herself a large glass of wine, waiting for him to return.

~

Josh walked through his front door, shutting out the guys standing watch on the pavement, already flicking through their digital cameras in search of a photo they could sell for a headline.

Silently he strode to the kitchen, knowing Sophie would be there, probably with a cup of tea, staring into the garden. He rounded the corner. She sat in her usual place, but with a glass of wine. She looked up at him when he walked in, a strained smile on her lips, dark circles under her eyes. She wasn't okay.

Wrapping her in a tight hug, he kissed her hair. She didn't need to say anything. This was all too much, and she was done. He could feel it seeping out of every fibre in her body. "Let me run you a bath," he said softly, taking her hand and walking her upstairs.

She sat on the sofa in his room while he ran the water, pouring in concoction after concoction to fill the bath with bubbles and the air with fragrance.

When the tub had been filled, he pulled her into the bathroom. "Take as much time as you need. I'll be in my studio."

"You're not joining me?" She swished the water. As tempting as it was to jump right in with her, she needed peace right now, and if he did get in, that was the last thing she'd get.

"No." He stroked her cheek. "I think you need some alone time. I'm just next door if you need me." He turned to walk away. "We'll stay at yours tomorrow." When he looked back at her from the door, she was already getting undressed.

She hadn't even put up a fight. He could tell that's what she wanted, she just didn't want to disappoint him. But he wasn't in the slightest. It was a strain on them both.

"Thank you," she said, relief on her face.

"We'll talk later, yeah?"

She nodded up at him in her underwear, a pale blue silky set. God, he could so easily stay here, but that wouldn't be helpful to her.

"Just shout if you need anything," he said, and then wrenched himself away from the door. He needed to write to take his mind off of her beautiful body soaking in bubbles, the hot water sliding over her skin.

Fuck. Now he was really regretting not getting in there with her.

He sat at his piano, obsessively playing the notes he'd been working on, again and again. It was good. But it wasn't perfect. Something was missing.

He'd been lost in his world for what only felt like minutes when warm hands slid down his chest and Sophie's scent mixed with bubble bath wrapped around him.

"I love that melody on the piano," she whispered, leaning her soft body on his back. She was pure heaven.

"It's so close to being finished. I can feel it."

"You're a perfectionist." She sat on the piano stool next to him. She had put her pyjamas on, and even covered in cotton trousers and a button-down shirt, she was still the most magnificent sight he had ever laid eyes on. Her blonde hair was dark and damp from her bath, pulled back into a ponytail.

"You weren't very long."

"I was more than an hour." She nudged him, smirking.

He had obviously completely lost track of time. "Do you play?" he asked as she felt the keys on the piano.

"I would've loved to have learnt to play an instrument. But my mum didn't have the time or the money." She shrugged.

"It's never too late to learn. Here." He lifted her hand and placed her fingers on the keys. "Your thumb starts on the 'c' note." He manipulated her fingers to rest on the remaining keys. "Relax your hand, try to press softly at first. The more you practice the smoother you will become." He laid his hand gently on hers. "C, c," he sang as they pressed the key with her thumb. Then he moved their fingers up. "G, g, a, a, g." The notes tinkled from the baby grand piano.

"Twinkle, Twinkle?" She raised an eyebrow at him. "Seriously?"

"Hey, at least you knew what you were playing. Everyone has to start somewhere. And Twinkle, Twinkle is as good as any place to start." He tapped the next notes with her fingers. "And now you can teach your kids at school how to play."

She rested her head against his shoulder. "That's a lovely idea, but I might have to teach them on a sheet of paper made to look like a keyboard. The school doesn't have enough budget to buy keyboards."

"I'll buy them then!" He tapped with their fingers, playing Twinkle, Twinkle over and over again, allowing her to learn the notes and melody, gently easing off the pressure of his own fingers until she was playing on her own without even realising it.

"You don't have to do that."

"I know I don't. But I'd like to. Being able to play and create is so important in childhood. Them learning something new, realising that they can achieve anything with practice and perseverance—it's a life skill. You can do all of that with keyboards. Or even a recorder. But I think your ears would appreciate keyboards more." He twisted a piece of her hair around his finger, thinking.

Why hadn't he thought before about supporting kids in learning to play instruments? If he hadn't learned the piano and guitar growing up, there was no way he could have achieved what he had. He'd loved music from an early age, and if his parents hadn't supported that he probably would have lost it. And then what? He wouldn't have written music. He wouldn't have travelled the world. And he wouldn't have met Sophie.

He snapped himself away from his thoughts. "You're playing on your own." He nodded at her hand that was still mindlessly playing the nursery rhyme.

As she looked down at her fingers, they tripped over themselves and the wrong note jarred.

"Well, almost anyway," she said, dropping her hand from the piano. "Thanks for teaching me."

"Anytime." He pulled her up and walked her over to the sofa, letting her lie back with him, resting her cheek on his chest. "Do you want to talk now?" he asked her softly.

She sighed heavily. "I've just had a bad day. The kids were playing up and then it's a long drive here." She sighed again. "And I don't like hiding coming here. Waiting for you to lead the paps away. I miss you greeting me when I get in from work."

"I know." He rubbed her shoulder. "I hate having to hide you. But we decided that so you wouldn't get in trouble at work."

"I know. And that was the right decision. I'm just bored of it." She twisted a small button on his shirt. "I'm bored of not being normal."

His heart seized. He was anything but normal. His life was anything but normal. If she wanted that, then he wasn't for her. What was she getting at?

"I just want to go for a walk with you without having to check we aren't being followed. To go for a nice dinner. To walk into your house like I'm your girlfriend and not a mistress."

"My girlfriend?" He pulled her chin up to look at him. They hadn't ever labelled this. And now that she had, it felt right. "I like the sound of that." He rubbed his thumb across her soft bottom lip.

"Sorry, I know we haven't said anything like that. It's just easier to say that than try to figure out another way to put it."

"I should've asked."

She shook her head. "That's not what this is about."

"I know it's not. But I still should've asked. I want you as my girlfriend. I want to shout out to the world that you're mine. But we can't right now. We have to give it some time."

He still hadn't told Sophie that he loved her. It had never felt like the right moment. He didn't want it to be some throwaway comment. He wanted it to be special, something she would always remember. But the more he thought about it, the more his gut twisted.

Right now, he could feel they were on the brink of something. He could sense it in her. As much as she may want this, she could easily walk away from him. And that meant he couldn't tell her he loved her now.

"You know I don't live a normal life," he said. "People think that anything I do, they should know about. That I'm public property. As much as I want to, I can't change that. This is what I was trying to protect you from."

She pushed up away from him. "What is it with you and protecting me? All I'm saying is I want to be normal with you. To go out and have fun."

"But if we get spotted and you end up in the papers again, you could lose your job."

"I know that." She slapped her hands on her thighs.

"So you want to risk it? For what? A meal in a swanky restaurant? To go to the cinema? What?" His heart thundered harder.

He didn't get it. What they had now was great. Yes, they had to do a few things to cover their tracks, and he was anything but thrilled by that. But they did it to protect themselves from the wolves outside. It was worth a bit of pain to keep them safe and happy. Wasn't it? Sophie clearly didn't think so.

"I spent years with a boyfriend who didn't want to go out with me to places. And now I have a boyfriend who can't go out with me. Can't you see how frustrated that makes me feel?"

Josh rubbed at his face, suddenly exhausted. He didn't get it. Not really. He didn't understand why she would push this.

"But you don't want to be in the papers, Sophie." He shook his head. He was between a rock and a hard place. "You want to go out and do all these things, but if we do that you'll be in the public eye. Journalists will start digging into you. People will turn up to take pictures of you. Let's just assume you don't lose your job. Do you really want that?"

He searched her face for the truth. If she was with him for the fame and the money, she had to go. No matter how much he had fallen for her. He couldn't be with another Emily.

"I can't change who I am," he continued. "If you want those things then you have to be prepared for the consequences. If you don't want those consequences, then we can't go out in public together. Or…" His stomach dropped, bile rising in his throat. He didn't want to say the alternative.

"Or?" she croaked, her eyes turning watery.

"You'll have to leave me." He didn't look at her. Couldn't. If she decided to walk away now he would be heartbroken. It would take all of his willpower to let her go. But he would have to, because she had decided it was the right thing for her. Forcing her to stay with him risked her happiness and her life.

"Is that what you want me to do?" She sat on the edge of the sofa, her hands in her lap.

"I want you to be happy. And if you aren't happy here, with me, then yes. That's what you would have to do."

"And you would want me to leave?" Her voice rose louder.

"Yes, if that's what—" Before he could finish speaking, she shot up from the sofa and stormed to the door.

She turned back to him. "I can't even storm out of here because of those idiots outside!" Then she slammed the door on him.

CHAPTER 23

Sophie lay in bed, eyes shut tightly, listening to Josh rustling around in the darkness. She had lain here for hours, waiting for him to finally come to bed. It was gone midnight and her tummy grumbled underneath the duvet.

She had slammed the studio door on him and stormed into the bedroom, not knowing where else to go. He hadn't come to get her. They didn't have dinner. So she had just sat in bed, playing on her phone, her anger gradually subsiding. But not enough to go back to him to apologise.

Thud.

"Shit," he whispered loudly. The bed dipped and bounced slightly. He must have stubbed his toe. "Can I turn the light on now? I know you're not asleep."

Sighing, she reached out for the bedside light. She had tried to go to sleep after putting down her phone, but her mind whirled and spun. So instead, she had just lain there, praying sleep would take her. Sitting up in bed, she rested against the headboard. Josh was examining his toe closely in the light.

"Is your toe okay?" she asked him.

"Well, despite the way it feels, it hasn't ripped off." He held it tightly.

"A bit over-dramatic."

He looked up at her. "Maybe."

His eyes were dark, his hair tousled. He stared at her. She stared back. Both silent. He lay across the bed, putting his head on her shoulder.

"I'm sorry," he whispered into her pyjamas.

"I'm sorry too." She rested her cheek on his messy hair.

"I don't like arguing with you."

"Me neither."

"I'll take you out, if that's really what you want. Maybe there's a place I can find where we won't be followed or spotted. But you have to know there's always a chance."

"I know." She scooted down the bed further, her eyes suddenly feeling heavy. "I'm prepared for that."

Josh turned her to face away from him, wrapping his arm around her hip, and pressing his front against her back. Now that she was in his arms, safe and warm, her eyes felt heavy and soon she was sleeping soundly. Not a care in the world.

Josh sat on Sophie's sofa, waiting. He'd spent all week trying to find the perfect place for a date for them. Another private dinner wouldn't cut the mustard. Sophie wanted him to prove that he liked her, wanted to be with her, that they were an item. He needed to prove that in front of people they didn't know, but make sure the press didn't find out.

Hopefully he would succeed. No matter what she'd said about being prepared if they were pictured together, he wasn't so sure that she was.

She walked down the stairs, her boots tapping on the bare floorboards. He rose from the sofa, straightening his shirt, and went to join her. She looked stunning as ever, in dark jeans and a thick jumper. She wrapped her scarf around her and pulled her coat on.

"You're going to want your gloves too." He shrugged his coat on, pulled on some gloves and put a flat cap on his head. She looked at him, probably realising that he was trying to hide. But he had to take as many precautions as he could.

"Where are we going?" she asked, grabbing her bag.

"You'll find out when we get there. It will be fun."

She chewed her lip, obviously not enjoying the element of surprise as much as she had the first time. He took her hand and led her out the door.

Not long later, Josh pulled his car into a dark car park lit at one end with floodlights that beckoned visitors to the entrance. The wheels of his Range Rover slipped in the mud. Josh parked and carefully picked his way through the muddy field to let Sophie out of the passenger door. She looked this way and that, trying to figure out where they were. A family group walked past them, talking and laughing.

"What is this place?" she asked as they walked the same way, both looking for the clearest route to take.

"You don't know?" He took her hand tentatively, forcing himself to not check around him before he did so. She shook her head, so he continued, "They do Halloween events here." They joined the queue to get into the farm and attractions.

"What?"

"You'll see."

He paid for their tickets and led her through the turnstiles under a banner saying Hauntfest. The courtyard was a hive of activity. Families and couples were walking between food stalls and small pop-up shops, and kids dressed in Halloween costumes were gobbling up sweets and toffee apples. There were some fairground rides, like dodgems and a Ferris wheel, but the main attractions were the haunted field, the tractor ride and the house of horrors.

"Right, where to first?"

"I have no idea." Her eyes scanned everywhere, trying to take it all in.

"Well, how much of a scaredy-cat are you?" he asked, looking at the map he'd been given.

"Erm…" Her hand tightened around his bicep.

"Quite a big scaredy-cat, then." He smiled at her, then looked back at the map. "Well, this field is only rated one spooky face. So let's try that first and work our way up." He led her to the haunted corn maze.

She snuggled into him, stealing his warmth as they waited in line to get into the maze. Screams echoed from within, and every now and then groups would exit yelling or laughing.

As they waited, Josh sneakily looked around them. No one was staring at him—they were all too busy chatting with their friends, or figuring out where to go next. This was perfect.

"Welcome to the Haunted Corn Field." They were greeted by a teenager dressed up in a clown costume holding a large plastic knife. "I'll let you in in a minute, I just have to give the group in front a head start. Follow the markers, don't cut through the cornstalks, and no running." He checked around the gate. Once he was satisfied he'd left enough time, he lifted the latch to let them through and said, "Most importantly, don't scream."

Josh laughed at how unenthusiastic the teenager was. "We'll try not to."

He held onto Sophie's shoulders and directed her into the maze. She bent her head low, as if trying not to see anything. "Nothing's going to hurt you." He hurried her up. The further they walked in the maze, the quieter the noise of the crowds became. They turned corner after corner, following the path and rope laid out for them. All they saw was corn.

Rustling sounded behind them. Sophie spun around. "What was that?" she asked, narrowing her eyes, looking between the tall stalks.

"Probably just wind. Come on, let's keep going." They walked a little further. It felt like they were in the middle of nowhere, surrounded by nothing but maize.

"Are you sure this is right? We haven't seen anyone or anything. I would have thought we'd at least have seen a pumpkin by now. Maybe we took a wrong turn."

Josh stopped and scanned around them. "We can't have done, there wasn't anywhere to go wrong."

The rustling sound started again. Sophie squished her body against his, her heart thumping against his bicep. "It's that sound again," she whispered. "Are we being followed?"

"We can't be." He went to step forward.

"Gotcha!" A masked figure jumped out at him, holding a chainsaw that started whirring loudly, his clothes dirty and torn. Sophie let out a high-pitched scream, her hand holding tight to his, dragging him with her.

"Run!" She suddenly sprinted away from them, flecks of mud splashing everywhere.

Josh followed her. "You shouldn't be running!" he yelled. The masked man with the chainsaw hobbled after them, one leg dragging behind. "But on second thoughts…" He ran and quickly caught up, holding her arm in case she fell. They twisted through the paths, putting as much distance between them and the hobbling mass murderer as they could.

They turned a corner and flew out into the bright lights of the courtyard. Only then did Sophie stop and hold onto him tightly. "That was horrible." She snuggled into his neck.

He chuckled, his heart beating just as fast as hers. "It wasn't that bad. Just one chainsaw-wielding murderer."

She slapped his chest. "We could've been hurt."

"Hardly," he laughed, shielding himself from another playful whack. "He didn't have a chain on it."

"He could've been any weirdo from the street, actually a murderer, just walking in and disguising himself as an actor."

"I'm sure he wasn't." He kissed her gently, letting her forget. "Come on. I'll get you a hot drink to make up for it." He pulled her towards the stalls, looking for something to warm them up.

They opted for hot chocolate with whipped cream and marshmallows in a paper cup. Maybe not the most luxurious thing he could have bought her, but right at that moment...it was perfect. They stood to one side, people watching.

It was a novelty to Josh. Normally he was the one being watched, but he still hadn't had one double take, one photograph or autograph request. He was starting to feel normal.

Had he found the one place on earth where no one recognised him? Maybe he needed to move here. Surely the paparazzi wouldn't bother driving down here every day? Why hadn't he moved to the countryside earlier?

Sophie started to look at a stall selling Halloween decorations. He slipped his hand into hers easily, enjoying the freedom of being able to act without fear of being seen or pictured. He could get used to this.

Wrapping his arm around her, he pulled her in close to him. "I like this," he whispered into her ear through her thick, blonde hair.

"What, being chased by a murderer?" she giggled. "You might have issues if that's the case."

He chuckled. "No. Being here with you. Not worrying about anything. Just us." He kissed her cheek. "Thanks for insisting we do something together."

She smiled up at him, pure joy in her eyes. "Remember that in future. I always know best."

"I'll remember." He pulled her away from the display. "I think it's time we do the tractor ride."

"No, let's just stay here and look at the stalls and eat and drink," she wrinkled her nose up, looking back longingly at the bright lights and stalls.

"You've already looked at all of them. Come on, it's only two spooky faces. Then I'll get you a hot dog or something."

Why would anyone pay to go here? Sophie jumped off the trailer, her hand clutching Josh's, shaking. Two scary faces her arse. That had been ten times worse than the maze. She knew it was only actors dressed up in scary costumes who had been following the tractor, tugging at their coats through the rails on the trailer, making loud bangs on the side. But she was sure she'd screamed more than the ten-year-old sitting next to her.

"Did you enjoy that?" Josh asked as they walked back to the safety of the courtyard. She definitely preferred it there.

"No! How can anyone enjoy that?" She ruffled her hair, dislodging some more of whatever the actors had thrown at them, pretending it was maggots. At least she hoped they were pretending. She shivered.

Josh pulled at something in her hair. "Rice, see?" He held up a little grain, that silly little smirk on his face.

"How are you not scared?" She pushed at his chest, annoyed at his bravery.

"It's all make-believe." His laugh was deep and hearty. It sent her insides to mush every time she heard it.

"Right, well, you owe me a hotdog. And a drink, I believe! An alcoholic one this time."

Laughing again, he pulled her against him, kissing her on the lips. Their first kiss in public. And he hadn't even looked round before he did it either. She melted.

"You're cute when you're scared." He nuzzled her nose.

"I hate you," she told him, not meaning it at all. She hid herself in the nook of his neck—she was safe there.

"No, you don't." He rubbed her back.

"No, I don't." She looked up at him, words on her lips they hadn't said yet.

He stared deep into her eyes, his own eyes almost turning black, a crooked little smile on his luscious lips. "Come on then," he eventually said, pulling her away from her thoughts.

They ordered a hotdog and a bottle of beer each and seated themselves at one of the picnic benches. Josh straddled the seat and Sophie sat in between Josh's legs on the bench. He traced shapes on her back as she finished eating, his eyes scanning the crowds. Would he ever not?

"Please relax," she whispered to him.

"I am." He picked up his beer and took a sip.

"You aren't. You're on edge again."

He sighed. "Well, I was relaxed. Now I just have that feeling we're being watched."

"I think all those creepy actors in the woods have got to you." She kissed him, hoping it would ease his tension. But he stopped their kiss at a peck. "Come on, no one has even given you a second glance," she whispered, aware of all the people that surrounded them also eating.

"Hmm." He looked at her then, his eyes softening as he saw how worried she was. "Sorry, Soph." He rubbed her cheek.

"Let's go and do this last thing then. How many scary faces does it have?"

He pulled the map from his pocket. "Three. Are you sure? We can give it a miss if you like?"

"No, it's fine. That one and we're done. Then nothing else scary for a whole year!" She got up from the bench.

"What, not even a scary movie?" He followed her up and placed their wrappers in the bin.

"Nope. Not even a scary movie." She wrapped her arms around him and rose on her tippy toes. He bent down and kissed her, wrapping his arms around her too.

She could get used to this.

Their kiss deepened and Josh could feel the low rumble from Sophie's moan. Maybe they could just go home and enjoy each other? As he pulled away from her to suggest it, he had that feeling they were being watched again.

He looked up over her head and froze.

A man was standing at the other end of the courtyard, staring at him. Even from this distance, there was no doubt he was looking at him, his eyes narrowed. It wasn't normal for him to be recognised by men—his fans were mostly women.

Uneasy, he tugged at Sophie's hand. "Come on then, I think we should just go home." He tried to pull her in the direction of the car, his stomach clenching. Something was wrong.

"No, you wanted to do the haunted house. Come on." Spinning in the opposite direction, Sophie led them to the attraction, Josh scanning the crowds for the man. But he was gone. And then he walked into Sophie's back.

She stood like a statue, her face frozen. Immediately, he saw what she was looking at. That man. He walked towards them and Sophie's hand slid from his.

"Are you fucking kidding me?" the man spat.

"Wh-what are you doing here?" she stuttered.

She knew this guy?

"What the fuck are you doing here?" He took another step towards her.

"Whoa!" Josh stepped around Sophie, blocking her from view. "Enough of the language, mate. You don't talk like that around a lady. And there are kids around."

"She ain't no lady. She's a fucking whore." He pointed around Josh to Sophie.

"Enough!" Josh pushed him in the chest, knocking him backwards slightly.

Who the hell was this jerk? The man tried to step around him again to speak to Sophie, but Josh mirrored him, shielding her shrinking form. They stood toe to toe, evenly matched in height, but Josh was broader.

"You seriously left me for this loser?"

Loser? He was many things, but he sure as hell wasn't that.

The man carried on. "Oh no, wait, you didn't leave me, did you? You cheated on me with him. And then lied to me!"

Shit! Was this her ex-boyfriend? Josh turned his head to Sophie, needing an explanation.

"I-I..." she stammered, seeming completely lost for words.

"You can't even deny it, can you? You told me you hadn't slept with this jerk, yet here you are sucking face, all over each other. You're a fucking liar."

Still Sophie said nothing, her mouth opening and closing, tears filling her eyes.

"Enough." Josh turned back to the bloke, shielding her again. He would deck him if he needed to. "No more. You don't get to shout at her like that. Walk away." He felt behind him to take Sophie's hand, ready to guide her back to the car.

"You don't get to tell me what to do." He jabbed his finger into Josh's chest.

Josh took his finger, bending it backwards, and pushed him away from them. "Back off!"

"Oh, you think you're so big, Mr Money Bags, Mr Big Shot. Well, you can have her. But I'd watch out for that money-grabbing bitch if I were you. She's a piece of work. Don't trust a fucking word that comes out of her mouth. She'll rinse you for everything you got." He scoffed. "She's had a long list of guys. You're not the first, and you sure as hell won't be the last."

Josh turned his back on the man and guided Sophie along in front of him. People stared at them as they left.

"She's only after you for your money," he called after them. "I bet she called those paps up herself to take her picture!"

CHAPTER 24

Josh's hand cradled her back as he guided her softly through the crowds, all eyes on them. And then she heard it. Whispers and mutterings.

"Isn't that Josh Heart?"

"Josh Heart is here."

"Ask him for a picture."

"I can't believe it's Josh Heart!"

Despite all the hushed words around them, Josh kept his eyes focused through the crowd, and Sophie blindly followed him. What on earth had just happened?

She had frozen when she saw Scott. How was he here? They had driven so far out, she didn't think she'd bump into anyone she knew. And then he'd started shouting and calling her names as everyone around them stared, parents pulling their kids away from the angry man. She couldn't even defend herself. She had just stood, gawping. Words tumbling around her head but none of them escaping.

She should have said that she hadn't cheated on him. She had split up with him before anything happened, and she and

Josh had only just got together. But he wouldn't have believed her. He wouldn't have listened.

Josh opened the car door for her, lifted her up into the tall seat, and slammed the door. Then he strode round to his side.

They drove in silence, the radio singing happy tunes. Why was he not saying anything? His knuckles were white on the steering wheel.

"Josh…" she eventually croaked.

"I think it's best to talk when we're back at your house," he said tersely.

Was he mad at her? What had she done? "Okay." She looked out of the window, the dark trees and bushes lining the country roads flashing past.

When they reached her house, Josh opened her car door for her. But his eyes didn't meet hers. Her tummy twisted.

She let them into the house, dreading what he was going to say. He was obviously mad at her. She placed her keys on the little console table, shrugged off her coat and pulled off her muddy boots. When she finally turned to look at Josh, he was still standing in his coat, boots and cute little flat cap, his face as hard as stone, his hands shoved deep in his pockets. He hadn't left her welcome mat.

"Aren't you taking your coat off?" she asked, her heart pounding in her chest. The most horrible feeling was filling every part of her body.

"No. I don't think there's any need." His jaw clenched.

"What's going on?" she asked, stepping towards him, her hand outstretched, the horrible feeling of dread multiplying.

"What's going on?" His tone made her wince and retreat. "I think you need to tell *me* what's going on. You haven't said a word. You haven't tried to explain. You haven't defended yourself."

"Defended myself? What do I need to defend myself against?"

"Everything your ex-boyfriend said. Assuming he was your ex-boyfriend. Because you haven't even told me who he was. Or is he telling the truth and you never actually dumped him?"

She stared at him, gobsmacked. He believed Scott. "Josh." She couldn't say another word. Her heart was shattering.

"And what else did he say?" He placed his finger on his lip. "Oh yes, that you're a liar, a cheater, a money-grabber, a fame-hunter. Am I missing anything?"

"You believe him? You seriously believe what he said?" How could he?

"You haven't said anything to even try to defend yourself. To make me not believe him."

And then she broke, anger splitting her usually timid temperament. Channelling her inner Belle, she exploded. "That's because I shouldn't have to! And I will not! I will not justify myself to him. Or to you. You shouldn't ask me to defend myself from lies. How can you even begin to think he's telling the truth?"

"Because you haven't said anything. Not one thing, Sophie. You just opened and closed your mouth like a bloody goldfish. You've obviously spun a web of lies. I've been here before, Sophie. I've been with someone who was only with me because of my name, my money, my influence. And she almost died. She got so sucked into this fantasy world. She changed from a down-to-earth girl, just like you, to a drug addict, constantly wanting to go out, to be treated, to be in the papers. And I can already see you morphing into her."

"What? What are you even talking about? You haven't ever mentioned anything about that."

"What, like you've mentioned all your past boyfriends," he scoffed, turning from her.

"Are you kidding me? I haven't been with anyone for ten years apart from Scott." Sophie slapped her hands against her thighs. How could she get through to him? "What do you mean, you can see me morphing into her?"

"You're already changing. You've already hidden things from me. You said yourself that you could quit your job and I would support you. You've already argued with me about going out. What's next? A fancy holiday? A new car?"

"I was joking about the job! I told you that! I haven't hidden anything from you. I don't want anything from you." He scoffed again at her. Then she realised. "You're never going to believe me, are you? What can I possibly say to you to make you believe me?"

He shrugged his shoulders. "I think your actions have spoken enough for me to see who you really are."

Her eyes filled with tears, which she commanded to not fall. Not yet anyway. "Then you need to leave. Right now. I don't want you in my house. How dare you insult me. I shouldn't have to prove myself to you. If you can't see that everything he said was a lie, and you believe it, then you don't know me at all. We're over." She turned from him so the tears in her eyes could drop, her heart stabbing with pain.

"Too right we are." And then the door unlatched and slammed closed. She collapsed on the floor, a pile of rubble, broken down by his mistrust.

CHAPTER 25

Sean threw a magazine down on Josh's studio coffee table. "You're going to want to look at that." He slumped onto the sofa.

"I don't need to, thank you."

Sean picked up the paper and chucked it at his head. "Look at it, will you?"

Josh looked up from his notes and grabbed the paper from the floor. Unsurprisingly, a picture of him was on the front page, a crappy, grainy photo of him and Sophie at the Hauntfest, kissing. The kiss they'd had right before he spotted her ex, wrongly thinking he was a fan. He threw the paper back on the floor.

"There's more on page four." Sean scrolled through his phone.

Sighing, Josh picked up the paper again, turning the pages. More photographs showed him wrapped around Sophie, snuggled against her, kissing her head. "And?"

"Did you read the headline?"

Josh turned back to the front page. *Money-grabbing cheat*

has her claws into British heartthrob. He scanned the article. An interview with Sophie's ex.

After Josh Heart released a statement the day after the Best of British Talent Awards ceremony denying any involvement with the contest winner Sophie Ward, pictures have emerged of them cosying up together at the Hauntfest event in a small village in Kent.

In an interview with Sophie's recent ex-boyfriend Scott Webb, he tells us how Sophie lied to him about spending the night with British singer and songwriter Josh Heart while they were still dating. Scott goes on to say Sophie is only with Josh Heart for his fame and money and that she almost bankrupted him with demands for expensive gifts and treats.

How did Josh fall for such a manipulative woman? Find out more on page four.

We can only hope Josh comes to his senses and leaves Sophie Ward in the dust.

Finally having enough, Josh chucked the paper in his bin and turned back to his writing.

"What's the bet she's lost her job?" Sean asked him.

"I don't care."

"That's pretty harsh, mate." Sean stood up and came to sit on the piano stool next to him, just where Sophie had sat all those nights ago. His gut twisted. He did care, he just didn't want to. "Are you putting anything out?"

He shook his head. His publicist had called last night, warning him of the impending story. She'd yelled at him for not telling her anything about Sophie. If she'd known, maybe she could've protected them, or diverted attention from them. But now there was nothing she could do. The story was being run no matter what.

"It didn't help last time," Josh said. "It won't help now either."

"So you're just throwing her to the wolves?" Sean looked at the papers in front of Josh.

"She played with them first."

Sean tutted at him. "You don't really believe any of that stuff, do you? None of it makes sense."

"Makes sense to me," Josh mumbled.

"Wow, mate. I knew Emily did a number on you, but I never thought you'd throw your life away because of something one crazy woman did. What happened with her was horrible. But you've got to see not everyone is out for your money." Josh didn't say anything. "I think you need to get out of the industry, mate, before you lose yourself and everything you care about."

"I'm not about to lose you, am I?"

"No, mate. You won't ever lose me. But you don't want me to keep your bed warm at night, do you?" Sean nudged him in the ribs.

"No. Maybe not. You're a bit too hairy for my liking."

Sean chuckled. "I think you need to give this whole thing a second thought. You almost lost Sophie once. Can you really bear to lose her again?"

Josh shrugged. He felt numbed by the whole thing. He couldn't allow himself to think about not seeing Sophie again, otherwise he might crack and he couldn't afford that. So all he did was write.

"Remember, I know you, mate," Sean added. "And I can read what you're writing."

"I was writing this before." Josh shuffled the papers with the song about Sophie, suddenly losing his train of thought. As much as he loved Sean, in times like this he was a pain in the arse.

"Course you were. Fancy going for a drink?"

Josh laughed at him. "The last time you took me for a drink, I accidentally bumped into Sophie. I can't chance that again."

Sean slapped him on the back. "Come on then, at least grab a beer with me downstairs."

~

Sophie sat in the staffroom for the last morning briefing of the half term. Next week couldn't come quickly enough. A whole week off. She needed it. She would spend all day, every day in bed.

Doodling on her notepad, she bounced her knee up and down, dreading what was coming next.

Claire addressed the room. "So our last bit for today's meeting is just to announce that Jennifer has been appointed as our next assistant head teacher." Everyone applauded and Jen stood up briefly to give a little wave. "It's very well deserved and something Jennifer has been striving for, for a very long time now."

Sophie almost choked on the mouthful of tea she had just sipped from her reusable cup.

Long time her arse. Everyone knew Sophie had been earmarked for that job. It was like they had waited for her to mess up again just so they could humiliate her. Not that she needed any more humiliation. She'd had more than her fair share for a lifetime.

"I'm sure you will all help Jennifer as she transitions into her role next term. Right, let's make today a good one." Everyone got up from their chairs, the legs scraping on the tiled floor.

Sophie grabbed her bag and when she turned round Jennifer was standing there, blocking her way. "Hi," Sophie said as she put her bag over her shoulder.

"Hi, Sophie. I just wanted to check you were okay."

"Yeah," Sophie lied. She was getting used to that. "Why wouldn't I be?"

187

Jennifer twisted her long, brown braid around her fingers. They had been quite friendly really. Well, maybe not so friendly that Sophie would have confided in her about how her heart was breaking into a million pieces and she'd had to buy two lots of concealer to cover her dark puffy eyes from all the sleepless nights. And certainly not friendly enough for Jennifer to have not stolen her promotion. But you know, friendly-ish.

"You know, because I got the promotion," Jen said.

Sophie wanted to throw up in her mouth. "No, I'm happy for you." *Liar.* "You'll do a great job." That wasn't a lie. But it wasn't easy to admit.

"Great. As long as there are no hard feelings." She turned around, leaving Sophie on her own while she went to join the senior leadership team.

No, there weren't any hard feelings against Jen. The headmistress, on the other hand…she was the one who had made the decision. Decided to believe what the papers had written about Sophie, as if she hadn't known her for the last eight years.

Sophie walked past the group, her head down. Claire patted Jennifer on the back. "She was the only candidate to be considered really. We're very lucky to have her."

Sophie's blood boiled. The only candidate. The *only* candidate. She let the door slam behind her. Claire had said that on purpose, knowing full well that Sophie was walking past, that Sophie had actually been the only candidate until she messed it up with a stupid relationship.

But that wasn't anyone else's business. She stomped down the hallway to her classroom, her skin hot to the touch from rage. So what if she had popped up in a newspaper twice? That didn't affect her ability to teach, or to manage, or to make key decisions for the school. What about when Claire had been caught doing the dirty in the stationery cupboard with the school janitor? Was she sacked? Nope! What about when Jennifer had sworn in front of her class? Did she get passed over for promotion? Obviously not.

Reaching her room, she slammed her books and bag down on her table. *Breathe in...breathe out. Calm yourself, Sophie. Stop acting like Belle. This will all blow over.*

Except it wouldn't. She could feel it. This school was done with her. They had made their decision. And now it was time for Sophie to make hers.

She quickly opened her laptop. There were fifteen minutes left before her class arrived. Pulling up her emails, she typed a letter—short, sweet and to the point.

To Claire,

Please take this email as notice of my resignation.

In light of recent events, it has become apparent to me that my fellow members of staff and managers do not know the person I really am, and I cannot work in this environment any longer. Therefore, I will be leaving the employment of this school. I will work until the term finishes at the Christmas break.

Sophie.

Her finger hovered over the button. She scanned the email. Did she have the guts to do this? To leave school? To leave *this* school, the one she had grown up in and attended herself?

Fuck it. Who cared anymore? Certainly not her.

She jabbed her finger on the Send button.

CHAPTER 26

Sophie had spent the whole of the half-term holiday wondering if she'd done the right thing, and she'd had to call Belle on a number of occasions to persuade her that she had. They had been back to school for a week now after the October half-term break. All of the students had been really sad to hear that she was leaving. So much so that Sophie had considered running to Claire to withdraw her resignation. But it was already done. Already set in motion.

Now a small knock on the door had Sophie turning her head. Jennifer stood at the open door.

"Carry on class, I will be one minute," Sophie said.

The students bent their heads again, carrying on writing their short stories. At least they were all behaving.

"There's a big delivery at reception with your name on it." Jennifer looked over Sophie's shoulder at the class, no doubt trying to find something wrong with what they were doing. She had become a bit of a tyrant since stepping into her new role.

"Oh, okay. I don't know what that could be."

"I'll stay with the class while you get it." She walked into the classroom and wandered around the tables, leaning over the children's shoulders and reading their work. Sophie sighed. Jennifer was hardly an approachable teacher. Not wanting to disrupt them any further, she left them to fend for themselves.

At reception, Cathy, the receptionist, was busy overseeing a delivery driver stacking large boxes. "What have you been ordering?" she asked Sophie.

Sophie looked over her shoulder at the delivery note. "Nothing. I can't think what this would even be."

"It came with this envelope addressed to you." Cathy handed her the envelope.

Dear Sophie,

Please find enclosed thirty keyboards for use at Winton Green Primary School, free of charge on behalf of The Heart Trust.

We have also enclosed some sheet music and some workbooks to help you and your pupils on your musical journey from Twinkle, Twinkle, Little Star and beyond.

Please contact us should you need anything.

The Heart Trust.

Sophie drew in a deep breath and clenched her jaw. *Josh.*

"What's The Heart Trust?" Cathy asked.

Sophie stuffed the letter back into the envelope. "Oh, nothing. It was just a grant I applied for, not thinking I would get it. I had completely forgotten about it." She planted a strained smile on her face.

She hadn't ever heard of The Heart Trust. But there wasn't a doubt in her mind that it was something to do with 'British heartthrob, Josh Heart'. She cringed, remembering the headlines that were seared in her mind.

"Nice one. You're getting pretty lucky with your competitions now." Cathy nudged her.

"Aren't I just? Can I come and sort them at lunchtime or do you need them moved now?"

"Lunch is fine. Go and save the young ones from the wicked witch." She sniggered. Cathy had never really liked Jennifer.

Sophie walked back to her class. What was she meant to do with thirty keyboards? Should she return them? There wasn't any doubt that the kids would love them, and after all, it was all about the kids.

She chewed her lip, confused as hell. Why would he have sent them? What did it mean?

In his home studio, Josh listened back to the final version of his latest song. He had rushed to record it last week without any notice. The song had bubbled about in his brain for weeks and he had to get it out or else his head would have exploded. This was the last thing that reminded him of Sophie. And it needed to be gone. Now he should be able to sleep at night.

He listened intently, his keen ear ready to spot the slightest issue, missed beat or bad editing.

Nothing. It was done. Finished. At last.

It was due to be released tomorrow without any notice. No press releases. No interviews. No heads-up. He'd never done it this way before, and his record label had been a bit dubious about it, but for him this wasn't about sales or getting to number one in the first week of release. It was about getting Sophie out of his head, and more importantly, his heart.

Suddenly needing to get out, away from those traitorous thoughts of running back to her and begging for forgiveness, he grabbed his jacket and a baseball cap, and shot out of his front door. He was in his car before the photographers even realised he was there and lifted their cameras to take a photo.

Not knowing where to go, he drove around London aimlessly, until he ended up near the place Emily used to live.

His heart dropped. They had spent many days and nights in those early weeks at her place, before she got lost in his world.

He parked the car on a nearly empty street, glancing around to make sure no one had followed him. Walking along the road, his baseball cap pulled low over his eyes and his shoulders hunched up to his ears, he braced himself against the brisk November wind.

On the corner of her street, they used to visit a little Italian restaurant where the waiters were a bit too chatty, but the food was divine. Now it had been turned into a trendy coffee shop, as almost all places in London had been.

He pushed open the door and stood in the short line. Why was he here? Had he meant to drive here? He hadn't thought he'd known where he was going, but maybe he'd meant to turn up here.

From the corner of his eye, he caught sight of a man looking at him. Great. He'd been spotted. Again.

Shifting his gaze further around, he looked at the man and his heart dropped. It was Emily's father, sitting in the corner with a cup of tea, a toastie and a newspaper. Josh didn't move, until the person behind him cleared their throat to signify he was next in line to order.

He ordered a coffee to go. Then, grabbing the cup, he walked over to Emily's dad, David. He wasn't sure what sort of welcome he'd get. David had never seemed like an angry man, but then again, Josh had never given him cause to be.

"Hi, David," he croaked.

"Josh." He nodded as if he couldn't quite believe Josh was standing in front of him. At least he hadn't greeted him with a punch. Yet. "I can't believe you're here."

"Me neither. I've been meaning to get in contact with you. But every time I go to call you, I stop myself."

David pointed to the chair opposite him. "Please sit. I'd really like to chat with you. If you have time, of course."

"I have time." Josh pulled out the chair and sat down, nursing his to-go cup in his cold hands. "I'm relieved you haven't shouted at me yet, in all honesty." He played with the tiny bit of cardboard that was wrapped around his cup.

"Shouted? Why would I have shouted?"

Josh gulped. "Everything that happened with..." He couldn't say her name, not to her father. He shook his head and shrugged. "I just expected you to be angry."

"I'm not angry, Josh. I expected you to leave when you saw me just now. So I guess that makes two of us walking on eggshells." He leant back in his chair. "I've been wanting to call you for a long time too, to talk to you about Emily."

Dread filled every bone in his body. What had happened to her? "Is she okay?"

"She's fine, Josh. Better than she's ever been before. With your help, she's finally drug free. And has been for a very long time." Josh let out the breath he'd been holding. "The battle is obviously not over, and it'll be a constant fight for her all her life. But we finally have our daughter back."

"I'm so glad to hear that. But I'm so sorry she met me and went down that path. Honestly, I was never into the scene and if I'd known earlier that she had started to do drugs, I would've stopped her."

"Josh, meeting you was not the problem. You must know that."

"But if she hadn't been at all those parties where it was easy to get hold of, she wouldn't have ended up like this."

"Josh." David leant forward and took hold of his forearm. "She was already in it. Did you not know that? She already had a drug problem, she'd just been able to hide it from everyone. Did she never tell you?"

Josh shook his head. So she hadn't taken to drugs because of the life they were living? It can't have helped, though.

David sighed, shifting in his seat. "Josh, I can see you're still trying to find a way to blame yourself. You're not responsible. You never were. This is Emily's fight. You couldn't have protected her from it. She hid it from you. If you'd known and tried to stop it, she still would've found a way to do it."

Was that true? Had she really hidden a drug addiction from him? So it wasn't his life that had poisoned her. The dread in his bones started to ebb away. His mouth was dry and a lump had formed in his throat.

"Without your help, your support, paying for her to go through the best rehab in the country, she wouldn't be here," David said. "She wants to say thank you to you. So does Helen. And so do I. We have our daughter back, because of you."

CHAPTER 27

"Come on, it's about time you looked at it." Belle shoved the magazine towards Sophie.

"I really don't want to. They sent it to me last week, and I've just ignored it. I can't. I don't need to. What good is going to come from looking at it?"

"You need to see it. Everyone else has. Look." Belle picked up the magazine and flicked through, finding the right page, bang in the middle. They were sitting on the sofa at Belle's place. "Besides them completely jumping on the bandwagon with all the pap pictures of you and Josh, this is a really good piece. You look stunning, and your interview was great." She shoved the page under Sophie's nose.

Sophie couldn't help it. She looked down, burning bile rising in her throat. The centrefold spread was covered with pictures from the awards night. Photos of Sophie alone and some of her with Josh. The most glorious pictures she had ever seen. She lifted the magazine, inspecting their faces.

The picture of them together, as if dancing, was exquisite. They had been standing still, but you would never know it— they looked as if they were dancing in a ballroom. Sophie was looking up at Josh, her face inches away from his. In that moment she'd felt as if he were going to kiss her, and she'd been disappointed when he didn't, thinking she was getting carried away with the moment. But the glint in Josh's eye—the one she'd come to know so well over those weeks they spent together—made it obvious. He had wanted her, even then. It was the same look that he had in the grainy picture Scott took of them at the Hauntfest and sold to the papers.

If only she could go back to that moment. She sighed. What would she do? Would she have kissed him? Taken the bull by the horns and skipped over all the mess? Or would she have walked away from him? Maybe not allowing him to walk her back to the hotel and refusing his offer to spend the night with him would have avoided all of this.

But did she really want to live in a world where she had missed what it was like to be loved by Josh? To live in a world where she thought that Scott was her true love? No. Even with all this pain, she would never choose that.

"You look sad." Belle handed her a large glass of wine.

Sitting back on the sofa, Sophie laid the magazine next to her, unable to look anymore. "I am. I hurt. All over. I'm exhausted and drained."

"Oh, Soph." Belle scooted next to her, pulling her in to rest on her shoulder. "I can't even imagine. I mean, I've had my fair share of breakups. But I've never been in love."

Love. The greatest reason to feel like crap. Love had brought them together. And fear had torn them apart.

"I miss him," her tears flowed freely, soaking Belle's shirt.

"I know you do."

"He sent thirty keyboards to the school."

Belle pushed her away so that she could look into her eyes, a frown creasing her forehead. "He did what?"

"Sent thirty keyboards for the school to use. For free. From

The Heart Trust. I googled it. He's set up a charity to encourage kids to learn an instrument."

"Oh, that's so sweet," Belle gushed.

"Don't say that's so sweet. Say it's a horrible thing to do. And how confusing that must be for me—what an arsehole for playing me around." Sophie took a large gulp of her drink.

"Well…" Belle scrunched up her nose. "None of that's true really, is it?"

Sophie slumped her head into her hands. "No," she moaned. Why was this so difficult? They were done. Over. Had been for two weeks now. Yet every second that passed by was harder to bear. Wasn't this meant to be getting easier?

"Those keyboards weren't about you and him, Soph. It's about the kids. And as their teacher, you know what a difference that will make. And not just to your kids, but to all the kids in the school." She topped their glasses up with more wine.

"Yes, I know." Sophie took another large gulp. Thankfully it was a Friday and she'd be sleeping at Belle's tonight.

"Bloody bugger that you won't be able to take them with you when you leave though. What a great way to convince someone to hire you."

"Hey! Surely people will hire me because I'm an amazing and talented teacher?" Sophie pouted. Her job search hadn't been successful so far.

"Well, yes." Belle patted her hand. "But with thirty keyboards too?" She blew out an exaggerated breath, sliding her hand through her long brown hair. "You would have been irresistible!"

"Maybe I'll have to sneak them out of the school in the dead of night then." Sophie chuckled, her body fizzing all over from the wine. The onset of drunk giggles was coming.

"I'll be there. Just give me a call."

And then they planned out what outfits they would wear

and what item of clothing would make the best balaclava. By the time they had a plan, they'd demolished the whole bottle of wine and were lounging on the floor, rolling with laughter.

～

Sophie was woken up by something sharp digging repeatedly in her ribs.

"Shit, Sophie, wake up! Sophie! Sophie, wake up."

"What?" she moaned, rolling away from her friend who was attacking her. Her head pounded. Blimey, what time had they ended up going to bed last night? She squinted one eye at Belle's alarm clock. Nine o'clock. She'd better be waking her up for a fried breakfast.

"Look at this." Belle held her phone in front of Sophie's eyes, but she recoiled from the bright light, shutting them tight.

"Too bright," she groaned, and shoved her head under the pillow. Why, oh why was she friends with someone who functioned so well with a hangover?

"Well, listen then."

Sophie lifted the pillow slightly to release her ear and lay there waiting for Belle to turn on whatever it was that was so important.

But we were never meant to be,
So I let you go so that you could be free,
And now my mind is full of thoughts of you and me,
Just know you're always with me.

Sophie sat bolt upright in bed. "Is that Josh?"

Belle nodded her head, frantically scrolling through her phone. "Yup. Says here that he released this last night without any notice. People are going mental."

"Have you listened to all of it?" Sophie's heart thumped in her chest.

Belle shook her head, not looking up from her phone. "I'm still trying to find the full version."

"What does it even mean? Like, is it about me? About us? Does he regret it ending?"

Belle looked up, concern in her eyes. "I don't know, Soph," she whispered.

CHAPTER 28

Josh sat with his agent and the record label executives in their office in London. He'd called a last-minute meeting, and now they were all looking at him as if Christmas had come early, wondering what genius idea he'd come up with this time. They'd lapped up the results of his unannounced song drop. At first they hadn't wanted to do it, trying to convince him to do the usual press circuits and build up anticipation. But Josh had been adamant. The song wasn't about that. It wasn't about what chart position it would hit or how many sales it would make.

And now the executives sat staring in wonder at him. But his agent Tricia knew, her face sombre and dark.

Geoffrey leant across the table. "Please tell us you've secretly recorded an album you want to drop with no notice too?"

Josh shook his head. "I'm retiring."

Their faces dropped. "What do you mean?" Christian asked.

He was a good bloke and Josh would miss working with

him. But he was done…finished. He couldn't keep living this life.

"I've made the decision that I don't want to keep doing this anymore. Getting photographed whenever I leave the house. It's affecting my life and relationships. I've done that for who knows how many years now, and I'm done." He shrugged, completely at peace with his decision. It had been a long time coming.

"But you've just released your biggest hit yet!" Geoffrey said. "You can't just quit when you're up. You're number one in the charts already. Release an album and that will shoot to number one too, I'm sure of it."

Josh wouldn't miss him so much. He was always about the money, the deals, what the next plan was.

"It's not about that for me. I didn't release that song to get a number one, I released it to get it out of my head. It was driving me insane."

"Look…" Tricia tried to back him up, but Geoffrey cut her off.

"Is this because of that woman? That Sophie?" he spat. "A good-for-nothing floozy who was chasing your money has got you quitting?"

Josh saw red, his anger bubbling over the surface, erupting. "Don't you dare speak about her like that." He thumped his fist on the black glass table top separating them.

"So it quite clearly is about her. Well done for throwing your career away for someone who was using you." He clapped sarcastically.

Before Josh could stand and jump across the table at the jerk, Christian hoisted Geoffrey from his seat by the elbow and escorted him from the room. "I think it's time you left. You aren't helping here." He pushed him out the door and closed it behind him, then leaned back against it so that Geoffrey couldn't walk back in. "I'm sorry about that, Josh.

That was really unprofessional of him, and I will make a complaint about his behaviour. This isn't about us, it's about you, and I respect your decision, for what it's worth. I get how tough it must be." He walked back to the table, looking happy that Geoffrey was gone. "And I met Sophie at the awards night. She didn't seem like any of those things they said about her in the paper. It was obvious they were all just vicious lies from the ex." He sat back in his chair with a sigh.

Vicious lies. Josh looked down at the table, focusing on a droplet of water that had dripped from the side of his cold glass.

Was it all lies? He gulped. Had he just thrown her to the side for a bunch of nonsense?

His throat stung. Sophie hadn't ever really given him concern that she was in it for his money. She had been happy with going out with him where no one recognised him, whereas Emily had wanted to stay in London and visit places she knew they would be spotted. But Sophie hadn't. She had just wanted to be a normal couple. And he'd wanted that too. *Shit.* What the fuck had he done?

"Are you okay, Josh? You've gone as white as a sheet." Tricia held his forearm, nudging him gently.

"I think I've messed up."

Christian sighed again. "Somehow I don't think you're talking about your retirement." Josh shook his head. Christian rested his forearms on the table and said, "Go and get her, Josh. Everything else doesn't matter if you don't have someone you love to share it with." He rose from his chair. "That's obviously off the record. Officially, I told you we want to keep you on and will do anything to convince you to stay in the industry." He walked around the table and shook Josh's hand. "What are you still doing here? Go get her."

He opened the door and Josh ran through.

Josh struggled to find a parking space at Winton Green Primary School. He'd turned up at exactly the wrong time— home time. But he couldn't wait a moment longer to talk to Sophie. Walking against the sea of students, he dove this way and that, dodging little boys with dirty knees, girls with messy plaits, and mums and dads hurrying them all along.

Finally breaking free from the crowds, he headed for the main reception. He had no idea where Sophie would be, but he would find her. Somehow.

The reception was eerily quiet and he was transported back twenty years to when he was in primary school. Why did schools all have the same smell, that same air about them? His heart beat a bit faster. Walking silently across the dark grey carpet, he headed for the doors opposite him.

Gripping the cold door handle, he froze when a small cough sounded behind him. "Can I help you?"

Fuck. What on earth was he going to do?

He turned round and turned on what he hoped was a charming smile. "Sorry, I just need to grab something from Ms Ward's classroom."

An older lady with greying hair surveyed him over the tops of her glasses. *Please don't recognise me.*

"And what would that be?" she asked.

He stopped holding his breath. "My nephew left his homework in there and couldn't be bothered to go back himself, the little rascal. My sister will kill me if I don't grab it."

"What's your nephew's name?"

Shit. This woman should be an interrogator. He searched his memory for a name. Any name. Just think of any goddamn boy's name. "Jack." Please let there be a Jack in her class.

The lady's stony face seemed to ease. "Ah, yes. He is a little rascal. Do you know where you're going?"

Was he about to get away with this? Amazing. "Well, Jack said along the corridor, but other than that, no."

"Yes, just along the corridor, and the year five classroom is on the left, just after the staffroom."

"Great. Thank you so much for your help." Josh turned and walked through the double doors, grateful that the lady hadn't been younger, otherwise she probably would have recognised him.

CHAPTER 29

Sophie sat at one of the tables in her classroom, squeezed onto a small chair, tracing her fingers over the keyboard keys. The kids had been loving their weekly music lessons—every kid in every year had. It was a joy to see their little faces light up as they grew in confidence.

She had been practising too, so that she could help the children out as much as possible. But her go-to was still Twinkle, Twinkle. She'd practised it so much that her fingers were no longer jittery and clunky on the keys, but rather smooth and elegant. She was becoming a real pro.

Her fingers glided over the keys and she closed her eyes, lost in the memory of being next to Josh, happy and safe—in love. And she had never even told him.

Over the past few weeks, the initial pain of him not believing her had changed. Added to it now was pain that she didn't get to see him anymore. Didn't get to snuggle with him on the sofa or chat about their days. She missed him with every fibre of her being. And now she wished that she had just been open with him, been honest about how she felt. That she'd just said Scott was lying about everything. Josh had run away because he was scared, and she had been scared too. And now they were left with nothing.

She was so lost in that memory that she could almost feel him sitting next to her, hear his breathing, smell his aftershave.

"You've been practising?"

She snapped her eyes open. Josh stood in the doorway, leaning against the frame, his arms crossed. Pure perfection. A gift from heaven. Surely a hallucination.

"What are you doing here?" She didn't think she would see him again. Her heart thumped a little harder and her palms grew clammy.

"I needed to see you." He didn't move.

"W-why?"

He moved into the room and closed the door behind him. She stood up from the little chair, keeping the table between them. She didn't trust herself around him. Her whole body yearned for him, for her to run into his arms. But she wasn't so sure he would open them for her.

"You got the keyboards, I see." He touched the one closest to him and played a tune. The one he'd worked on all the weeks they were together. The one he released when they split up. His best hit yet.

A lump suddenly appeared in her throat. "Yes. The kids have been loving them."

Why was he here? Why was he not meeting her eye?

"They're lucky to have you as a teacher."

She sighed and turned her back on him, heading to her laptop to pack it away. "They won't be having me for much longer."

"What do you mean?" He had moved closer—she could sense him behind her. But she wouldn't turn to him.

"I've resigned. I have to work till the end of the term and then I'm gone." She choked on the words. She would miss these kids—miss this school. It was like a second home to her.

"I'm sorry, Soph." Josh felt for her fingers but she pulled them away from him.

"You should be. They passed me over for promotion because of you. I couldn't stay here anymore, Josh. The looks I get, the whispering behind my back. It's like people have forgotten they knew me and what sort of person I was. And they believed everything that was written about me. I can't be here anymore."

He gripped her hand tightly so that she couldn't pull away. As soon as he turned her around, she lost all her bravado. She collapsed in his arms, tears leaking down her cheeks. She hurt so much. From her head down to her toes. From work, from the press, from everything that had been written about her. From Josh. She pushed away from him, not wanting to take his comfort.

"Sophie, don't you think that out of anyone, I'm the one who knows what you're going through?"

"You're the reason, Josh."

"I know I'm the reason, goddammit!" He pushed his thumb and forefinger into his eyes and breathed heavily. After a second he looked at her, his eyes red. "I wish I wasn't this man, Sophie, this man who everyone knows. Who everyone thinks they have some claim on. That I was normal. But if I was normal, I wouldn't have met you. I wouldn't know what it's like to be with you, to have you as my friend, my supporter, my partner. I've tried living without you, Sophie. And every day was worse than the one before. And I can't do it anymore. I need you. I miss you. I fucked up. Again. When I promised I wouldn't. When I promised I would spend every day making up for my first mistake. God, I fucked up." He stepped towards her, tears streaking down his cheeks.

She stepped back from him, not sure if she should trust his words. Words were cheap. Words meant nothing.

"Sophie, I have so much I need to tell you. So much to explain. But this isn't the right place. Can we go home to talk?" He shook his head. "I mean your home."

Home. Did he see her home as his? It sure hadn't felt like home since he left. She nodded. "I need to pack away these keyboards first and gather some bits to take home."

"You gather, I'll put away." Just as she was about to turn from him, he swept a strand of hair from her face. "I've missed you so much," he whispered.

Her heart ached. She had missed him too and she couldn't deny that having him here, right this second, had already eased her pain. But she couldn't tell him that. Not yet.

Thankfully he turned from her first and started tidying the keyboards away onto the music trolleys, while she gathered her laptop and work.

Then they went down the corridor together, her hand twitching to reach out for his. But she wouldn't let herself take his hand, no matter how much she wanted to. Her body and soul longed for him, but she couldn't just brush everything under the carpet.

They walked side by side, her heart thundering in her ears. God, she'd missed him. Every muscle seemed to ache for him. His fingers brushed against hers as they walked, the gentlest touch, but it was on purpose. It had to be. His little finger twisted around hers, and she clung onto it, suddenly feeling so much better.

She sighed, her muscles easing, her heartbeat slowing, as if this was where she was meant to be and everything before had been survival mode. They pushed open the double doors to the reception area.

"You found her then?"

Sophie wrenched her fingers away from Josh like

lightning, her heart in her mouth. Cathy. She was like a hawk —nothing got past her.

"Yes, thank you." Josh smiled at her.

He was charming and so rugged. Although now, looking at him again, Sophie thought he seemed tired—his eyes dark, his hair longer than normal and stubble coating his cheeks. She had never seen him with stubble—he'd always been clean-shaven. He looked back at her, searching her eyes, looking for an answer.

She frowned at him. What was he doing?

His face settled into a contented smile and with a soft sigh he turned back to Cathy. "I'm sorry, but I lied to you when I said I needed to grab something for my nephew. I'm Josh." He held his hand out for Cathy to shake. What was he doing? "Josh Heart."

Cathy shook his hand. "I knew who you were, Josh. You're quite well known around here now. And besides, there is no Jack in Sophie's class." She laughed.

Sophie looked between the two of them, with no clue what was happening.

"But thank you for being honest with me," Cathy added. "I thought if you took the trouble to make up a whole story, then you must have needed to speak to Sophie pretty urgently. Have you two sorted it all out?"

"I'm hoping we're getting there." Josh turned to Sophie, a twinkle in his eye, and reached for her hand again.

"Good. She's been miserable these last couple of weeks."

"Me too."

"Erm…" Sophie was so lost, like she was stuck in some sort of alternate dimension. "We should go." God forbid they got caught here by Claire. Although, really, there wasn't anything Claire could do about it, seeing as she had already resigned.

"I'll see you tomorrow then, Sophie." Cathy winked at her. "Oh, and thanks for the keyboards, Josh."

"My pleasure." Josh tugged Sophie's hand and they walked out of the building together. "I'll walk you to your car and then catch you at home."

Sophie pointed towards the staff car park and Josh walked confidently with her, his strides long and quick. He wasn't looking around them for cameras or fans, he wasn't even wearing a hat to shield himself. And he'd been so open with Cathy about who he was. What had happened to him?

～

Josh knocked on Sophie's door, his heart in his mouth. This felt big. Huge. His whole future depended on laying everything on the line with her. Telling her everything. About Emily, about his fears, about his retirement and about his hopes.

Sophie opened the door, tentatively looking round at him. He wanted to pull her to him, kiss her, wrap his arms around her, run his fingers through her soft hair. But he had to tread carefully. She was hurt and upset. She was wary of him. And she had every reason to be.

He stepped past her into the hallway and let her close the door behind them.

"Do you want a drink?" she asked, squeezing back past him in the tight hallway. Her body felt heavenly up against his. And the light in her eyes told him she felt exactly the same.

"A coffee would be great." He followed her into the kitchen. "So you've resigned?"

"Yes." She busied herself making the coffee. "I never thought I'd leave, but I couldn't be there anymore." She sounded sad. His heart hurt for her.

"Have you got another job?"

She shook her head, sighing. "Nothing yet."

"You'll find something. I know you will."

"I don't know if I will. What do I say for the reason I left my last school? Everyone will know about me. When I was at secondary school, we had a teacher who everyone said had been moved on from his last school because he'd sold cigarettes to a student. He couldn't shake the reputation—everyone talked about it behind his back. And it probably wasn't even true. I don't want to be that teacher."

"Something will work out, Sophie."

She handed him his cup of coffee and walked past him to the living room with her own, careful to not touch him like she had in the hallway.

Walking with her, past her cluttered dining table, Josh recognised his own pile of papers, neatly stacked in the corner. "I'd forgotten these were here." He leafed through the papers with his early notes for the song he'd just released. They were all from his time here with Sophie, about how content he had felt.

Sophie sat on her sofa while he looked through the pile. In the middle of the stack was the speech he'd written the day everyone came over, when Tony told him to tell Sophie how he felt. And he never had. Now he read it through. Right at the bottom, next to a purple stamp that said good work, was a scribble he hadn't put there. *I love you too.*

Sophie. Sophie had written that. She had read his speech declaring his love for her, and she loved him back. But they had never told each other.

"When did you see this?" He held the piece of paper up.

"What even is it?" She squinted at it.

"My speech to you. Where I wrote how I felt about you. About us."

She shrugged and brought her feet up underneath her on her sofa. "I don't remember it." She stared out of the window, drinking her coffee.

"Don't lie. You're a terrible liar. When did you read it?"

She shrugged again. "I don't know. Sometime before you left. When did you write it?"

He sat next to her on the sofa. Why had they made this so difficult? "The night everyone came over. Tony told me how he regretted not telling Jodie sooner that he loved her—that they had made it so complicated and before he knew it, he'd almost lost her. He warned me. And I didn't listen. I got scared and I didn't tell you. And then I messed it up and lost you."

"You didn't need to tell me. You showed me. I could feel it."

"But I should have told you. I should've been honest. I loved you. I still love you. I think I did from the moment I saw you." He stroked her cheek. A tear spilled from her eye and he wiped it away. "I'm so sorry, Sophie. I wish I could turn back time and do things differently. I know what Scott said about you is all lies. I didn't give you the chance to tell your side of the story." That wasn't right. He shook his head. "No, you didn't need to tell me your side. I should've just believed you. Should've known he was lying, and trusted you without doubt. I think I was just so scared. Scared that this was too good to be true. That I didn't deserve this. That something bad would happen. And then something bad did happen….because I made it."

"Josh…"

"No, Sophie, I have so much to say. So much to tell you." He dropped her hand and rested his elbows on his knees. It was time to lay it all out on the table. He drew in a deep breath.

"When I was with Emily, she transformed in front of my eyes. From this sweet, innocent thing, who wouldn't say boo to a goose, to someone who craved attention and the limelight. She constantly pushed to go out to dinner, to only eat at the finest restaurants, to accept all the party invites I got. She wanted to be seen—needed to be. Everything Scott said you were, she was. But I never knew. Not until it was too late. And before long, she was doing drugs—hard-core drugs. All the time. And then one day…"

He sucked in a deep, shuddering breath. Sophie gripped his hand.

Drawing strength from her touch, he continued. "One day, I went to her flat and found her—in her bed, the curtains closed, the room stale. She had overdosed and was unconscious. I called the ambulance and they came, after what felt like years. They wheeled her out and I couldn't see her for hours. I had to call up her parents to tell them. It was the worst call I've ever made. How do you tell someone their child may die? That she had started doing drugs because of the world I lived in? We sat in the waiting room in silence. Waiting. And waiting. She was in intensive care for a week. We didn't leave her side apart from going home to shower and grabbing something to eat. We hardly said anything to each other. I knew that they blamed me, that I was the reason their little girl was in that place.

"I stayed with her for weeks after she woke up. But then she told me that we needed to end. That she wasn't in love with me. That she never really had been. She just loved the idea of me, of being with a celebrity, with my music. She loved the lifestyle, the glamorous parties, the money. But she hadn't loved me. And she couldn't continue to be with me, surrounded by all of that. She needed to heal—to rehabilitate. So I paid for her to attend a rehab program, the best in the country. I paid her parents every month so they could be off work and look after her. I paid off their mortgage so they didn't have to worry. And I stayed away."

"Oh, Josh." Sophie leant against him, holding him close. "I'm so sorry you went through all of that. Did she recover?"

"Well, I never knew. Until the other day. I ended up in a coffee shop near her home, and her dad was there. I thought he would shout at me, or throw a punch at me, or at least walk away. But we sat and talked. And he told me how she's doing. How she's stayed clean and is still attending her meetings to keep up her sobriety. But he also told me that she had been battling drug addiction for a long time—since long before I met her. She'd never told me—I didn't even have an inkling. So it wasn't because of me that she had entered that life. It was already a battle she was facing. And now it makes sense. It makes sense why she broke up with me, why she was even with me in the first place. Our relationship was all lies. All lies fuelled by her addiction."

"And how does that make you feel?"

"I don't know, really. I've lived for so long with the belief that it was my fault, and I set rules about never getting close to fans ever again. I couldn't risk someone else's life. That's why I tried to stay away from you. That's why I thought I had to protect you."

"Josh…do you know I'm actually not a mega fan of yours?" Sophie nibbled her lip.

"What do you mean?"

"I've always liked your music, but I haven't ever been to a concert of yours. I don't think I even have one of your albums. I entered that competition to go to the awards ceremony, not to meet you. That was just a bonus."

Josh's heart sank and then lifted. He chuckled. "You're kidding, right? All this time I thought you were a huge fan of mine. That you just loved the idea of me, not actually me. But you weren't. God, we could have saved ourselves so much trouble." He wrapped her in a hug, never having felt happier that someone wasn't a fan.

"I heard your latest song. The people on the radio said it's your best yet."

Josh nodded against her head. "You know it's about you, right?"

Sophie shifted, nestling herself further into the crook of his neck.

He lifted her chin so their eyes met. "Sophie, it's about you." She needed to believe him if they were to move forward. "It's a mix of what I wrote after we first met, what it felt like when we were together, and my dreams for us and our future. *Our* future, Sophie." His thumb caressed softly over her chin, along her jaw. "Since the moment I met you, everything has been about you. And I wouldn't have it any other way."

Sophie's eyes filled with tears, and a smile tumbled onto her lips.

Nearly all the tension seemed to leave Josh's body. She believed him. They could begin their life together with everything out in the open. Almost.

She sealed their happiness with a kiss. "Do you feel better now?" she asked when they broke apart.

"There's more." He sighed. "I've retired." He held his breath, waiting for her reaction.

He hadn't retired for her. He'd done it for himself—for his future. So that he could feel remotely like a normal human being again. Somewhere in the back of his mind he'd thought maybe he could move to the countryside. Life was so much simpler here, and people either didn't recognise him or didn't care. Maybe he could move here with Sophie.

Her eyebrows were drawn together. "Why?" she looked at him as if her whole world depended on his answer.

He stroked her cheek. "Not for you, Sophie. For me."

He drank her in—her beautiful golden hair shining in the winter sunlight that streamed through the window, her bright blue eyes, and her delicate hands that were fiddling with her top.

"I don't want the intrusion anymore. I want to be normal and not worry when I walk out the door. I want to be with the woman I love and not worry about how she feels being in the public eye. I don't want to be told what I have to do by industry specialists or my agent. I want to be me."

"So what will you do?"

He shrugged. "I'm not sure. And I don't care, really. Sitting around here in my pants all day sounds great." He laughed, nudging her. "But if you don't want that, I can still write songs for other people. And I want to do more with The Heart Trust. I want to encourage disadvantaged kids to pick up an instrument."

And then it came to him, what he really wanted for his future. Like a bolt of lightning right to his heart.

"And if all else fails, I'll just be your husband, here to support you, to look after you, to be your shoulder to cry on, the one you run to when you have a problem. The one you look for when you succeed. The one you laugh with. That's enough for me. I'm not asking you to marry me tomorrow. And God, I don't even have a ring. But I want you to be my wife when you want me to be your husband."

She threw herself on him with such force that they were sent backwards, ending up lying on the sofa with Sophie giggling in his ear.

"That is the most perfect thing I've ever heard. I have never wanted something so much in my life." She kissed him. "I've missed you so much."

"I've missed you so much, too. I'm so sorry, Sophie. For everything. I feel like I've messed everything up from start to finish. I already told you before that I would make it up to you every day. And I didn't. I messed up again."

"Josh," she whispered, nuzzling his nose. "Nobody is perfect. Our relationship certainly isn't perfect. We will upset each other again in the future, no matter how much we promise each other we won't. All we can do is try our best to love each other through good times and bad. And I promise to do that." She kissed the tip of his nose.

"I promise to do that, too. And I'll never run away again. Some things are worth holding on to. Like you, Sophie; I just can't let you go."

He squeezed her tight, kissing her. His body had missed her so much and having her pressed against him was doing him no good.

"Shit." He rested his forehead on hers. "I've got to talk to your brother."

She groaned, rubbing her hands over his chest. "Really? Do you have to?"

"Well…" He nibbled her ear through her hair. "It can wait for a bit."

Then he picked her up in one swoop, her squeals filling the room, her legs kicking wildly in the air. He slapped her bum playfully and carried her upstairs to have his wicked way with her.

CHAPTER 30

Sophie held Josh's hand as she pushed open the door to the pub. She had very reluctantly agreed to go so that Josh could talk to John. She would have preferred to stay in bed all night with him and order a takeaway. But Josh had insisted. Apparently it was his duty to apologise to John for treating her badly—again—and make it all okay. But she couldn't care less. She was happy. That's all that mattered.

The moment she walked through the door, John's face lit up…and then quickly fell as he saw who was behind her. She squeezed Josh's hand just a little tighter.

She hesitated in the doorway, unsure whether to walk straight up to the bar, or go and grab a table. Before she could decide, Josh led her to the bar. John stood on the other side, his jaw clenched, the muscles in his tattooed arms tight.

"John, I need to talk to you," Josh said.

John eyed him, not saying a word.

"I've got this, John." Tony got up from where he'd been sitting at the other end of the bar with Jodie, watching the showdown, and walked behind it to cover for John.

John chucked his tea towel on the bar top and walked out of the pub, Josh following behind closely.

At a complete loss now for what to do, Sophie joined Jodie. Tony poured her a large glass of white wine.

"What on earth is going on?" Jodie whispered, checking over her shoulder to where John and Josh had gone out.

"Josh showed up at school and we talked. He apologised and we made up. Then he said he needed to sort it out with John. Make it right."

Tony nodded, leaning against the bar, his eyes trained on the door.

"John's not going to punch him, is he?"

Tony took her hand, squeezing it tight. "No. He won't punch him. Just let them sort it between themselves. It's just what has to be done."

Her knee bounced up and down. Max sat next to her, demanding a stroke, and the action calmed her nerves. Slightly.

"He never said anything to Scott. So why's he bothered with Josh?"

"I think that's why," Tony replied. "He doesn't want history to repeat itself."

She scoffed. *Men.* "History isn't repeating itself. Scott never loved me, not really. And I didn't really love him. This is completely different."

"Well, you've got to admit that you two have had a pretty rocky start." Tony raised an eyebrow.

"Oh, right, because you and Jodie were plain sailing from the beginning, yeah?" *Bloody men.*

He held his hands up in defeat. "You're right! I won't judge. You're getting just as feisty as Belle these days." He went to serve a waiting customer.

Jodie leant in closer to her. "Everything will be fine. They both love you. They both want what's best for you. They'll sort it." She held her glass up for Sophie to clink. "Cheers. To a happily ever after."

Sophie dinged her glass with Jodie's. "To a happily ever after." That's if her brother didn't throttle her boyfriend.

Eventually, when Sophie's large glass of wine had been fully drunk, John walked through the door, his face unreadable. She stopped dead. Where was Josh?

He came in two seconds after John and winked at her as their eyes met. *Phew.* John walked over to her, kissed her on the forehead, and then retreated behind the bar without saying a word. He whipped the tea towel back over his shoulder and poured Josh a pint of beer.

Josh stood next to her, wrapping his arm around her back, and pulled her close. "Nothing to worry about," he whispered into her ear as John went about serving other customers.

"What happened?" she whispered back.

"Nothing. All you need to know is that everything is sorted. So you can relax. We can grab a table in a minute, if you like?"

She huffed. She really wanted to know everything that had been said out there. But the look in Josh's eye told her she wasn't about to get any answers. So instead, she snuggled into his chest and breathed him in. Surely she would get used to this?

No, she never would. They would argue and they would annoy each other. But without a shadow of a doubt, this was the man she was meant to be with for the rest of her life. The man she would marry, the man she would have children with. And nothing could stop the smile on her face. Nothing at all.

EPILOGUE

Belle's arm wrapped around Sophie's as they walked to The Dog, and pulled her in tightly to share each other's warmth. Sophie shivered. Why hadn't they got Josh to drive them? The evening was already pitch black and it had started to drizzle.

"Come on, grumpy. You're meant to be cheering me up. Put a smile on your face." Belle jiggled her arm up and down to warm them up some more. They'd be frozen by the time they got there.

"Sorry. It's been an emotional day."

"I know." They walked some more in silence.

It had been Sophie's last day at Winton Green Primary School, and she'd barely managed to keep herself from crying all day. And then, at the end of the school day, the children all stood up and read her a poem they had written to say thank you and goodbye. Some of them even played her a song they had composed with the keyboards Josh had donated. It was all she could do to not collapse in a heap of tears. Now her eyes filled up again.

Belle sighed, seeing Sophie overcome with emotion once more. "Oh, come on. Tonight is about celebrating."

"Yes, I know." She'd found a new job in a neighbouring village. It was only a short drive away and the kids seemed lovely. To top it all off, she had finally got that promotion and was now an assistant head teacher.

Despite all of that though, right now, she just longed to be going home to Josh, to snuggle in bed and watch a movie and let him make her forget the emotional day she'd had. But she couldn't say that to Belle. Not when Belle had sounded so desperate to go out together—alone.

"Anyway." Belle nudged her. "You should be feeling sorry for me. Not the other way around."

"Oh? And why is that?"

"Because Scarlet called me today."

Sophie groaned. Scarlet was Belle's 'best friend' from university. Apart from the fact that the two seemed to be constantly locked in a battle of one-upmanship. "What now?"

"She's sent out the invites to her wedding."

"When is it?"

"February. Barf. Apparently they got a last-minute deal on their dream venue because the couple who've had that date booked for the last three years have just split up."

"Oh, that's sad."

"For the couple or for me?"

Sophie laughed. "For the couple."

Belle sighed. "I know. And it means I have to find a date in the next two months. What's the likelihood of that?" She bent her head low.

As much of a front as Belle put on, Sophie knew she was lonely and had always wanted to find someone special. And going to Scarlet's wedding without a plus one would be an absolute no-go. She would rather be in a—what had Belle said?—she would rather be in a six-foot hole in the ground, surrounded by snakes and bugs, and force-fed Marmite on crackers for the rest of her life. Sophie had almost wet herself with laughter when she heard that. Belle always had hated Marmite.

"No one on the horizon?"

"Nope. How am I going to cope for a whole weekend with Scarlet, with no date and the bloody 'poor single Belle' eyes she gives me? Not to mention those bloody pity hugs where she pats me on the back and says 'oh, I'm sorry to hear it didn't work out, maybe next time.'"

"Why are you even friends with her, let alone agreeing to be her bridesmaid?"

"Right now I'm questioning that myself."

"I'm sure something will come up. And if not, is it really that bad if you don't have a date?"

Belle shot her the look of all looks, her eyes like daggers, her jaw as hard as stone. Obviously it would be the worst thing in the world.

They rounded the last corner and the pub sat in front of them, all lit up in the night.

"They better have the fire on. I'm frozen. I can't feel my fingers." Belle rubbed her hands together fiercely as they stopped at the door. "Go on." She nudged Sophie forward. "You go first."

Sophie pushed the door open and was met by a loud, "Surprise!"

All around her stood friends and family. Even Sean was there, along with Josh's parents and sister. They were all wearing silly hats and glasses, with balloons strewn around them. Homemade banners hung from the walls and the bar that said "Happy Leaving Day". And in the middle of it all stood Josh, his arms out wide, a big, silly grin on his handsome face, a party hat on his head.

She ran into his opened arms and hugged him tight. He swung her around in the air and she squeaked with delight. "Did you do this?" she asked when he put her down.

"Of course. You deserve a party." And he handed her a glass of champagne from the bar.

"I can't believe you organised this. And kept it a secret from me." She batted his chest.

"Well, I had help from John and your friends. You didn't make it easy, mind you. But we're here now and that's all that matters." He kissed her gently.

Sophie looked around all the smiling faces. Tony and Jodie were sitting at the bar, Max beside them as always, with John talking to them. For once in his life, he was on this side of the bar. Belle had gone to see her brother, Adam, who was talking to James. And there were even some of her work colleagues here, the ones who hadn't believed a word the papers had said.

She squeezed Josh's hand. "Thank you so much. This means the world to me." She kissed him once more and then they went to celebrate with everyone.

Josh stood at the bar, his elbows resting on top of it. Sophie was talking to Belle, Adam and James, laughing with them, happy and content. As she laughed, her golden hair bounced in soft curls that she had done just for tonight.

This past month, he'd spent every minute at Sophie's house. And he hadn't looked back. This was where he was meant to be. With Sophie. His song had broken records and stayed at the top of the charts. But he didn't care. It hadn't changed his mind on his retirement, and all of the money from the record had gone to charity and helping to fund the first shipment of instruments to schools for students to use for music lessons. And he had Sophie to thank for that. Without her, he never would have realised how important it was to him.

Tony came to stand next to him. "You alright?" He slapped Josh on the back before settling back against the bar with him.

"Yeah. You?"

"Not too bad. You're not going to chicken out this time, are you?" Tony crossed his arms and looked towards Sophie.

"What do you mean?"

"I mean that ring burning a hole in your pocket."

Josh snapped his head round to Tony, his heart in his mouth. "How did you know?" He patted his pocket to check it was still there.

"Calm down. I can just tell something's up, and you keep touching your pocket. I just put two and two together."

Josh blew out his breath. "Does Soph…"

"No." Tony shook his head and rested his elbows leaning on the dark wood. "Sophie doesn't know anything. No one does. Just don't chicken out of it like you did when you were meant to tell her you loved her."

"I won't." Josh gulped. "Anyway, why are you lecturing me when you haven't done the same thing?"

Tony looked over at Jodie sitting on the bar stool, Max's head on her leg. "That will come. But for now we have other things going on." Jodie yawned.

Sophie broke away from Belle and started walking towards them. Tony patted him on the back and winked at him. "Good luck," he whispered, barely moving his lips. And he left to sit with Jodie again.

"Is he alright?" Sophie cuddled Josh, her eyes on Tony and Jodie. "Jodie worries me. She looks awfully tired at the moment. I think she's pushing herself too much."

"I think they're fine. He would have said something by now if not." Josh had a little inkling that they had big things on the horizon, due in just a few months' time. Sophie leant against the bar, twirling her glass on the top. "Sophie?" He took her hand in his. "I have something for you."

"You didn't have to get me anything." She bumped him with her hip.

"I did." He took the ring box from his pocket, opened it up and held it out to her, their backs shielding them from the view of everyone else. Their own private sanctuary, surrounded by all her loved ones. "I love you, Sophie. Nothing is going to change that. I want to spend the rest of my life with you. Will you marry me?"

Sophie looked up at him, her eyes glistening. "Of course I will!" They slipped the ring on her finger together—a beautiful, bespoke platinum band with yellow diamonds. And she threw her arms around him and kissed him.

The End

Want to hear more from the residents of Winton Green?
Sign up for Marie Harper Wright's Exclusive Reader List.
https://www.marieharperwright.com/exclusive-reader-list

Book 1 of the Winton Green series, No Promises, is available to buy now.

Book 3 of the Winton Green series…

Fake Promises

Fooling everyone that they're in love was easy. Not believing their own lie was nearly impossible.

Belle Johnson needed a date. There was no way she could show up to her friend's wedding without. If she did, she'd never live down the shame of everyone knowing she was single...again. Only one person was crazy enough to agree to be her pretend boyfriend for the week of the wedding, and that person was her brother's best friend. The plan was simple...until it wasn't. She wasn't meant to be sharing a bed with him, and she certainly shouldn't be waking up in his arms. But no matter how hard she tries, she just can't resist the one man she can't have.

James Wilson doesn't do commitment. He loves women, but only for one night. That is, until his best friend's sister runs to him like her life depends on it and kisses him like no one's watching. When he offered his fake boyfriend services, he hadn't counted on a week-long wedding celebration. Worse still, he actually likes kissing Belle. If he gives in to temptation with her, he will lose the only stable family he's ever known.

Belle and James are so convincing at being in love that they begin to fall for their own lie. But when they return home to real life, and the village of Winton Green, they worry that if people find out about their relationship they could lose everything, including each other.

Return to Winton Green in Fake Promises to find out if Belle and James will ever discover that love can never be faked.

Sign up to Marie Harper Wright's Exclusive Reader List to be the first to receive update's on Belle's and James's story, *Fake Promises*
https://www.marieharperwright.com/exclusive-reader-list

ABOUT THE AUTHOR

Marie Harper Wright lives and writes in Kent, UK with her husband and two boys. She wants to transport you to English countryside where you can forget all your troubles and lose yourself in picturesque villages with sassy heroines and loving heroes.

Find out more about Marie Harper Wright by signing up to her newsletter or by following her on social media.

www.marieharperwright.com